Tom Bryan was born in Manitoba, Canada in 1950. His father was of Irish stock, his mother a war bride from Penicuik. Tom has lived most of his adult life in Scotland and is currently writer-in-residence for the Borders, based in Selkirk. Tom is a poet with two published collections to date (*Wolfwind*, Chapman, 1996 and *North East Passage*, Scottish Cultural Press, 1996). He has also published several short stories and has had fiction broadcast on BBC Radio. His writing was shortlisted for the 1998 *Macallan/Scotland on Sunday* short story competition.

Tom was editor of *Northwords*, *The Broken Fiddle*, and currently edits *The Eildon Tree*.

www.11-9.co.uk

The Wolfclaw Chronicles

Tom Bryan

First published by

303a The Pentagon Centre
36 Washington Street
GLASGOW
G3 8AZ
Tel: 0141-204-1109
Fax: 0141-221-5363
E-mail: info@nwp.sol.co.uk
http://www.11-9.co.uk

11:9 is funded by the Scottish Arts
Council National Lottery Fund.

ISBN 1-903238-10-2

Typeset in Utopia
Designed by Mark Blackadder

Printed by WS Bookwell, Finland

*This book is dedicated to
the memory of my parents:*

*O.W. Bryan 1912-1953
Betty Bryan 1923-1972*

For Michael and Anna.

*With thanks to:
my agent Barbara McLean,
for keeping the faith.
To Val who helped
me get to this point.
To friends who gave
encouragement and advice,
particularly to Anne MacLeod
for the idea and to Elspeth
and Morelle for reading the mss.
Special thanks are due to
Robert Alan Jamieson
for valuable technical suggestions.
Finally, to all those people
who fight for the land and its
people and wildlife but
are not intimidated by wealth
and privilege; to those who can
be angry but still love.*

Chapter one

Cree Dan: We were all born that night. The night Ivan Murmansk put his dark hand on the bar of the Haddock Arms Hotel and waved his fish-gutting knife above it, saying: 'I vill kut ziz ov zo hellup me iv evver I vould betray you.' The mackerel blade shimmered above his fist, but the tension eased ... he withdrew his hand, then quietly put the knife away.

Thus 'Wolfclaw' was born, a howling wild clan:

Ivan himself, mackerel gutter on the good ship *Rasputin*, nine days out of Murmansk, missing his wife Anish and daughter Sura, pressed tightly together in photographs in a hard leather wallet in Ivan's back pocket. Ivan, whose English sounded like a chainsaw badly over-lubricated, dripping oil over every consonant – 'dozh, dozh, zhizhin, zhizhin, tsts, tsts, ushka, tootka.' All this in the stench and ming of the Haddock Arms, where Conger Mackenzie once said a person could fall asleep pissed and wake up in Shanghai or find himself in the hold of a diabolic Bulgarian Klondyker stripped to his y-fronts. Smoky purple haze above the heads, dark smoky wood from the holds of dead ships; beards and ganseys looming in and out of the sickly sweet odour of lager, rum and whisky: all wafted by the smell of sulphurous farts, stale puke and urine. The occasional tourist pops a clean head inside, only to withdraw it quickly in spasms of coughing. Tables of burnished wood where once Ivan's swarthy hand lay.

It was a night in mid-November. The Haddock Arms faced the pier and a row of houses, smoored now by the rain and hail, the curve of their light fading like a dying torch. Macqueensport – maybe a fiction to you but real enough to us in the dying days of our millennium—the 'first winter of the next Ice Age' said one punter looking into the steam of a pint glass. And who was born (or, reborn) that cold November night when all the world was shivering in the freezing fog outside?

I, Cree Dan, was ... but more about me later.

Killybegs: kicked off an Irish trawler for general laziness, plays the mandolin so badly that tourists buy him drinks not to play it at all ... who quotes the Easter Proclamation backwards, can recite all of Christy Moore's songs and enlivens pub crack with snatches of the philosophy of Sir Boyle Roche, the great eighteenth-century Irish eccentric. His favourite quote from Sir Boyle: 'The greatest of all possible misfortunes is usually followed by an even greater.' Or, 'Why should we do anything for posterity for what did posterity ever do for us?' Killybegs, a slender dark oil slick.

Local Highland lad, Conger, who must have a surname somewhere. Mackenzie, Macleod, Macdonald, Macrae. Short and muscular like a conger, so-called because years before, lobster fishing with his uncle, a giant conger eel flipped down the front of his gansey and almost into the nether regions of his oilskin trousers; the boy punched the huge eel in the head, knocking it unconscious far out into the sea. Conger's way of doing things: direct action. It would come in handy.

And Vratchken: a lassie in her late-twenties who was born locally but grew up in Buchan, working for a fish-selling company. Hair like raven-black steel wool and legs that did not stop. 'Vratchken', because a 'vratch' in Buchan is a spoiled child, someone always up to mischief, a two-thousand-year-old word for brat and 'ken', ye ken. Her Buchan auntie would say often enough, 'That quine is a vratch, ken?' And so the name stuck. Vratchken strode the pier and sorted out problems with mackerel and herring, cod and haddock, lobsters and prawns, in Russian, in Bulgarian, in Gaelic and most difficult of all, in broad Buchan as most of the ships were north-east trawlers.

That night in the pub, Vratchken spoke first. Vratch rattled away in English, mixed and blended with her own Buchan tongue, shifting as the hearer demanded or protested. 'Faa's wrang. Ess nae a funeral, ken?' We kent but it was the beginning of a bad joke: a Russian, Irishman, Highlander, half-breed and North Easter sat around a bar in mid-November in a dying place: aye, no jobs, houses, future and if Christ doesn't come at the toll of midnight in two years' time, then somebody else better save us. And it won't be Tombstone Tormod.

Tombstone is an island man, in fact, he is a man-island. He drives fish lorries when there are fish. When there are no fish, he has a bass player, guitarist and drummer and dark Tormod looks like a circus big top in his soiled red flannel shirt, a man-mountain who knows every song from *Cailin-mo-Runsa* to *Stand by yer Man* but he was now belting out *Boone was the Terror of Highway Number One*. The night was not going clearly at all. If we had too much to drink it was Vratchken's fault who was trying to start something: 'Win aff yer deid arses an div somethin aboot et ... '

A team. A clan. A secret society. Team. Pack, ken?

Killybegs: 'We'll be just like the Fianna Supermen. Truth, justice and the Macqueensport way. Robbing the rich to give to the poor, giving succour to widows, helping the needy in our own fashion, comforting the flotsam and jetsam of post-Thatcher Britain.'

Conger measures his speech the way he turns a net for repair, turning it over slowly many times then pushing it along for the next mending, in speech slower than a heron's flight: 'Absentee landlordism, white settlerism, agoraphobia, holiday homes ... but where to start man, where to start? Even if we teamed up, what about espionage man, fifth columns, informants. Betrayal ... ?' He didn't finish. Maybe Ivan only understood that one word and that's when Ivan made his threat (or promise).

Much later, Vratchken took her own sharp blade

out, a fisher quine's curve. She drew a small circle across her knuckle. 'Bleed brithers ... sisters' and drank, we all did the same, pressing each cut to the other: Cree Dan, Vratchken, Conger, Killybegs and Ivan; only Ivan did his with a claw he had on his necklace, first holding it up to Conger's lighter to sterilise it: 'Volk – Wolf – a wolf's claw.' And that was it. How 'Wolfclaw' came into being in the howling wind and hail. Lord, it must be hailing all over the world.

I Cree Dan, write all this down:

Wolfclaw Chronicles:

first minutes of the first meeting, general concern voiced at the general state of things in the last years of the second millennium; in Macqueensport, North West Scotland, Planet Earth, Milky Way, etc. Agreed we are, men and women of action, that we know earth, wind, fire and water. Housing, trees, nuclear dumping, landlords, feudalism, jobs, midges, horizontal rain, poaching; real acts, symbolic acts, defiant acts in order to raise awareness. Macqueensport? Souls of Mackenzies, Macleods, Macraes, Macdonalds, fishing, crofting, shopkeeping. Some Brummies, Cockneys, Scousers, Kanucks, Aussies, Kiwis, Eastern Europeans, Hebrideans, North-Easters, Glaswegians, alcoholics, religious mullahs, Rangers supporters, Aberdeen supporters. Folks getting older, young leaving, houses going as second homes, people of soul and grit being squeezed out, tribal divisions strong and deep, fish going, jobs going. Back to Macqueen. He supposedly killed the last wolf in Scotland so they named a town for him! A town with the blood of Scotland's last wolf on its hands; a bad omen, no honour in that.

Macqueen was a stalker to Mackintosh of Mackintosh and was commanded to stalk and kill a black beast which had killed two children. Macqueen found the wolf along the Findhorn River and:

'I foregathered wi the beast. My long dog there turned him. I buckled wi him, and dirkit him, and syne

whuttled his craig, and brought awa his countenance for fear he should come alive again ... '

> *Last wolf Macqueen?*

> *Wolfmen howling under Orion. Black she-wolf howling in Cree, Gaelic, Inuit, under lee of birch and rowan. Wrong. The last wolf howls in the village named after the slayer of the last wolf. Contradiction Macqueen? All of us who live in the wind and rain know about contradiction. My soul is split in two by it. I am Cree Dan, half-Cree and half-Gael and I have seen wolves and heard them howl. 'For fear he should come alive again.'*

> *Too late.*

> *Sorry, Macqueen, but the last wolf in Scotland is not* dead yet.

Chapter two
CREE DAN'S SONG

I was born in Grace Hospital, Winnipeg, Manitoba, Canada. My father, Donald Macrae, was born just down the street from the Haddock Arms. My mother was half-Cree, half-Assiniboine, born in a lumber camp near Flin Flon, Manitoba. They say the day I was born, the Red and Assiniboine Rivers were flooding and frothing with snowmelt. Dark mud, white foam. Maybe best for me, made of dark and light; two rivers foaming and struggling, but finally flowing side by side. Two rivers from different sources.

The dark side of it. Faces of burnished copper, oil dark hair, song words rising and falling, round faces in the space around me; words warm and fresh, cold and clear.

The light side of it. Faces mottled like red berries against a sudden autumn snow, eyes flecked blue and green like fish scales. Words in Gaelic and measured English, rising at the end.

Both clacking in my head. (Later, I saw two mountain goats fighting, clanging their horns like bells in the Rocky Mountain quiet – just like the languages inside my head.)

He will be a fine boy, Mary. *A' bhailaich mhor.*

Daniel is a good name, eh? It will go well with the boy, eh?

A river flowing from the west merges with a river flowing to the north; white water and red water.

All this in the pastel safety of baby boom Canada after the war, in houses identical, back yards flooded from hoses put through windows from kitchen sinks to form ice rinks from one end of the street to the other.

I saw:

Shirts and trousers frozen into blocks of ice.

Assiniboine and Blackfoot boys who chanted and disappeared like dying shadows behind mounds of frozen bulldozed earth.

Finns behind pastel walls: cigarette-making machines, rolling twenty roll-ups out onto the carpet, put on leather jackets, off to the Legion.

Ukrainians: coffee splashes on the *Ukrainian News*, blotting each word. On frozen mornings, children blonder than snow, trekking to school under the weight of real fur brought from Russia generations before.

And French-speaking boys; small, jagged and dark, like angry bees buzzing, stinging, disappearing.

Three languages clacking in my head, down the street to the school where a soft dark woman dressed in mauve, named Russula O'Flanagan, made me want to be a poet.

My old man left home when I was nine, leaving a note in Gaelic for my mother:

'I am going west. I am sorry. *Is mise, Domhnall.*'

I had much Gaelic by the time I was eighteen but refused the language because of my old man's desertion so I spoke to my mother in her own tongue or in English. I was supposed to be going to Toronto to University. I was sitting in the Greyhound Bus Station. A very fat white man loomed in front of me.

'Hey, you, Injun, move your ass I want to sit there.'

The bus station was nearly deserted. There were empty seats everywhere. I was tired so I moved two rows away. He followed.

'Hey, Injun, I want to sit there too.'

I said quietly. 'Your ass is fat enough, I suppose it can sit in every seat at once.'

'What did you say, Injun?' He took a drunken swing at me, missing and falling down. His head cracked hard on the floor, blood spilling from his ear. Two guys were sweeping the floor. They were speaking Gaelic to one another.

'It is not his fault, Malcolm, the fat boy started it.'

'Then let him run. We can only tell the police the dark boy was attacked first.'

'But I think the fat lad is surely killed.'

Surely. I panicked and ran. I awoke in Detroit on a shining September day. It was the start of a slow dream.

Dear Mary,

I write with much pain and embarrassment. I who was going to University to study languages to add to the three which already give me such trouble. I who have never understood the difference between spoken Cree and Assiniboine. Anyway, I got into trouble in the bus station but panicked and fled down here. Please don't worry for me, mother. I wasn't really ready for study but want to live a bit, maybe like the old man.

The Yanks are OK. Work is easy to find. Straight cash. I live in a huge boarding house surrounded by maple trees. Maybe it could be Winnipeg for all that. The winter was not so bad (which is not like Winnipeg) I could say I am learning to be a cooper, turning a lathe on staves of white oak, charred for the bourbon industry. The factory is in a clover field. I work in a quiet corner, near a big window covered in cobwebs. I wear safety gloves and goggles. The staves are in hoops which I shave with the sharp blade until they become as marble in my fingers. So, I would like to be a poet and maybe, come home again soon.

Your, Dan.

So, son of mine. A deal is struck, eh? If you do not worry about me, I will not worry about you. That is all I care for. I am not so lonely. Your father was always something of a wanderer. My own people understand that. It is no crime. He sends money. He has always done that, in fact, he sends most of his money. I am thinking of returning to my

own people in the north and it is there you should go
when you come back. You were also right to run, in
Toronto you would have no chance; maybe soon that will
change. Them geese that fly over make me lonely as death
for my own people. I have been dreaming of wolves lately.
I hear them above the din of the Finns' motorbikes. The
wolves are red and sleek. I don't know about the dreams of
white men; surely they can not dream of wolves who have
never seen them. I think your father dreamed in Gaelic. He
said he dreamed only about fish, women and railroad
tracks. Maybe too, setting suns.
My boy, take care of yourself.

>With much love, Mary

•   •   •   •   •   •   •   •   •   •   •   •   •   •   •   •   •   •   •

I signed on to paint water towers that spring, all over the
prairies from Mississippi to the flat sunflower fields of
Kansas.

'Cree Dan, what do you think?'

'The sunflowers remind me of home but it is still
cold there now, the snow is still melting into the rivers.'

There were four of us. Trotline, from down south,
skinny and tattooed with cobras. He headed the crew, gave
orders.

Choctaw, a white boy from Illinois.

Corndog and myself.

'Choctaw, you and Dan work from the stage,
Corndog, you can slide the rods later but do your seat work
first on the four legs. Well boys, up you go.'

Sunflowers to the horizon, the small town in a
checkerboard of early corn; redwing blackbird song rose up
to the tower.

Corndog whistled. 'Here I go down boys, thank the
Lord for good steel.' Corndog goes over the rail, eases himself
into the swing seat like a man dipping a toe in a hot bath.

Choctaw has fit a steel brace onto the ball atop the tank, in order to rig the stage at both ends. Each of us has a rope to untie and tie again, as we lower ourselves down.

We are painting the tower a robin's egg blue. Choctaw on one end of the stage. I am on the other. His hard hat is red, mine white. T-shirts and jeans under the prairie sun. Paint buckets are fixed to each side of our stage with bent coat-hangers. We are a few hundred feet up, at eye level with church steeples and grain elevators. People and cars move slowly below, shimmering in the sun.

We are ready to move, in unison we clutch our two ropes to ease the stage down until we tie them off again, arresting the stage where we want it. But my rope slips, the stage end snags on the tower and I am sliding off the stage to the ground two hundred feet below. Choctaw is on the stage now, clawing into my t-shirt, deflecting my fall enough to land me safely on the catwalk. My hard hat, paint and bucket thump on the grass below.

'Man, those sunflowers look real good. Choctaw, there are no wolves here. I must go where there are wolves.'

'You dumb fucker, you must have banged your head. Let's go for a cold beer. Enough adventure for one day. Shit, man, look at that paint on the grass.'

It looked like thick blood.

•   •   •   •   •   •   •   •   •   •   •   •   •   •   •   •   •

I was orphaned by a general delivery letter on Route 66, on the way to Missouri. I was twenty-one.

Dear Dan,
I am your mother's sister Gabrielle Boniface. I live in Flin Flon. Mary stayed with us for several months and was glad to be up north again. She spent a lot of time in the woods, going to places we both knew as children. She helped with the salmon smoking. She was unwell in the lungs – cancer – and

she died last week.

> *Your father Donald was killed last fall out in Medicine Hat in a farming accident at harvest time. He was buried there.*

> *You know your name in our tongue is 'Next to Last Wolf'. It is a long story, best told by us, eh?*

> *Dan, you are kin and most welcome to live with me and my husband and children. Your mother spoke proudly of you but was never worried for you, thinking this is your own journey. A 'salmon coming home' she said. I am sorry to give you this bad news.*

> *Sincerely,*
> *Gabrielle Boniface*

I lie in a Highway 66 motel under a wash of neon. Heavy rigs roll by all night, going west to St.Louis. I fall asleep at dawn, a dream wolf howling in my ears.

Their graves are alike though a whole prairie apart. Willow slough, sweet prairie grass undulating in the wind, on hills which rise only inches in miles of contour. In my mother's language she is buried in 'The Place of the Sad Willows'. The Blackfeet call the place of my father's grave 'The Place of the White Birches'.

'*I Donald John Macrae leave my son Daniel ownership of the public house which I have inherited in turn from my own brother. It is known locally as the 'Haddock Arms'. It is in Macqueensport, Scotland.*

With it he inherits the adjoining outbuildings. To my wife Mary, I bequeath everything else. Farewell, I am, Donald John Macrae, Medicine Hat, Alberta, Canada.'

I have now been the sole proprietor and part-time barman of that inheritance for twenty-one years and will shuffle into the next millennium with that albatross wrapped lovingly around my neck. It sometimes chokes me. I have thought of changing its name to the Albatross Arms, or the Next to Last Wolf but there is still time for that

Chapter three

Late November and the hail is ripping in from the sea. The Haddock Arms is deserted. I am behind the bar when the door bursts open, the hail scattering on the hard floor like gunshot. It is crunched underfoot as the Wolfclaw Clan bustle in.

'Hail, hail, the hail is here, what the hail do we care, what the hail do we care ... '

Killybegs shouts in falsetto, leading the way to the 'Function Room' known locally as the 'Ruction Room'. A long table in a long room with a dark four-inch thick door of hard Canadian Pine. There are stuffed ferox trout in glass cases on each of the walls along with huge green glass jars with peacock feathers and dried feathery plants sticking out from them.

Around the table: Ivan florid face, head topped by a green wool toorie, red beard glistening with hail. Vratchken, dark brooding face, eyes like a bird's, darting, gathering data for the future, missing nothing, filing this feathered and fished room away in her tidy east/west mind, Doric and English, no doubt some Gaelic mixed in.

Killybegs (Darra Fillan) slick like a drop of dark ink, bushy eye brows, heavy eyelids; a lizard, a dark lizard, languid and asleep but nervous and tense underneath the sly sleepy humour.

Conger: thinning hair always exposed to the elements therefore of uncertain Highland colour: red, blond, dark, remarkable blue eyes with a shiny film over them, making them change colours like a chameleon, now grey, now light blue, now dark, like the seas off Macqueensport.

I opened. 'Wolfclaw, therefore, let's get into wolves. Communal, canny, perfect in a tribe but inspiring fear, hatred. Slinking, sly, slavering, rapid, fanged, werewolf legends. Define the wolf, we define ourselves and the work we will do.'

Vratchken, impatient. 'Fits aa ess shite? Wolf history? Ah hivna i time.'

Killybegs was shifting in his seat too.

'Ivan is first,' I said.

'The volk ... the wolf ... is no coward. I hear them. I have seen them. They are just dogs dancing around the edges of the forest. They creep. They know everything. It is simple. We be as the wolf. Keeping together, dancing around the edges. Hide. Blend into the wind, rain and snow. Attack as a team, cover our tracks. Just singing dogs.'

Vratchken added, 'Aye, wolf as symbol. Mah granny said they eesed tae hunt wolves in i city o Aiberdeen in i days o King Malcolm. A bittie afore her time, bit no muckle afore.'

'Wasting their time looking for handouts in Aberdeen,' said Conger, emptying a pint.

The hail rattled the window in the Function Room. The wind whistled.

A voice came from the bar. 'Can a freezing man get a drink in here?' I got up to serve the lone voice.

'Fits Dan aan aboot? Bluidy wolves. Killybegs, you're aafa seelent i nicht.'

'Cree Dan is leading up to something. He's wanting to paint the broad picture, then work ideas around it. A good symbol anyway. Listen, my granda once told me he heard in his own childhood of an old farmer coming across a wolf and her cubs in the Kerry mountains a hundred years after the "last wolf" in Ireland supposedly disappeared. The old farmer left them be and told only a few people about them.'

Vratchken was scowling. The hail rattled outside.

'We're getting somewhere slowly,' I said. 'Trust me, this is important.'

Ivan began again. 'The wolf is a dog, a gentle dog. All our dogs came from them. I fed wolves by hand as a boy.

The wolf *is* the Russian people. I knew old peasants who kept them as pets. Stalin wanted to exterminate the wolf. He slaughtered nearly fifty thousand wolves in the year after the war ended. My father remembered the huge fires of burning wolf flesh. He said the the Russian nation will die when the last wolf is killed there. The last wolf ... '

'Aye, in Banffshire in 1644.'

'In Ireland, in 1766.'

'In the Highlands in 1743.'

We learned a lot about wolves as the hail rattled the windows. The small circle of people in the room was eerie in the shadow of ostrich feathers and gigantic stuffed trout. We looked like sailors in a storm-tossed hold or early Christians under the protective sign of the fish.

I kept talking. 'Wolf as teamwork, canny, camouflage, song, survivor, victim. People cleared for sheep, sheep cleared for deer, deer cleared for wolves, wolves cleared for people. Wolf in sheep's clothing. I don't think it's been a waste of time. We'll see anyway.'

I saw them walk out into the cold night, Vratchken last, her unclasped hair winging in the wind, studded with shining ice. I turned each light off in turn, leaving all the glasses on the table, something I never usually do. I wanted to get upstairs to write.

Wolfclaw Chronicles

The Cree and Assiniboine knew their spirit helpers and the wolf was one, called by many names: shirker, singer, laugher, thief. The Gaels were just as good on the wolf: bleidire = mouth, hence bletherer. Breac = brindled. Faol, allabhair. Ruadh-chu = red dog.

*A Sutherland map made for Edward II: '**Hic abundant lupi**.'*

*1283: King Alexander III budgeted a position at Stirling for: '**ane hunter of wolves**.'*

1427: Royal Proclamation: 'The woolfe and woolfe brood suld be slaine.'

1428: King James I declared: 'that ilk baron sall chase and seek the quhelpes of Wolves and gar slay them.'

24 October, 1491: 'The treasure of Scotland paid five shillings to a fellow that brought King James IV two wolves in Linlithgow.'

1491: 'Spittals' established in Scotland for travellers to shelter at night against wolves, eg Spittal of Glenshee.

1527: Hector Boece: 'The wolffis are richt noisum to the time bestiall in all parts of Scotland ... '

Bishop Leslie of Ross, 1590: 'Our nychbour Inglande has nocht ane wolf ... but now nocht few, ye contrare, verie monie and maist cruel, chieflie in our North countrey, quhair nocht only invade they scheip, oxne, ye and horse, but evin men, specialie women with barne, outragiouslie and fercelle thay ovirthrows.'

1594: Six horses were killed by wolves on a Breadalbane farm.

1618: Taylor's 'Pennyles Pilgrimage' I saw in the Brea of Marr wolves and such like creatures which made me doubt I should never see a house again.'

1621: In Sutherland 'Six poundis threttein shillings four pennies given this yeeir to Thomas Gordoun, for the killing of ane wolff ... '

Then a solution was found. Burn the forests and you kill the wolves so up went the retreats of hazel, oak and birch, hawthorn, elm and willow, elder, alder, rowan and ancient pine.

Wolf killings fewer, wider apart. Kirkmichael, Banff, 1644. Killiecrankie by Ewen Cameron in 1680 and Glen Loth, Sutherland, 1700.

And Macqueen.

Maybe his heart wasn't in it. Macqueen was a stalker, a man not given to exaggeration. But the laird said a black beast had killed two children and Macqueen had to get the laird off his back. Macqueen stayed away all day and the Laird was apoplectic. These stalkers, what? Useless fellows given over to claret, sloth, drink and debauchery. That's my province. Where is he, man?

Macqueen strides in, tosses a bloody wolf head at the Laird's feet.

'As ah cam through thi slochd by east thi hill there, ah forgaithirt wi thi beast. My lang dog there turned him. Ah buckled wi him, dirkit him, an syne whuttled his craig, an brought awa his countenance for fear he might come alive again, for they are precarious creatures.'

Not the words of a braggart or exterminator. A man with a job to do and bairns to feed. He carried on with his duties, generally did as he was telt, died and had a village named for him. Macqueen leaves history then – no comment – the last wolf. Macqueen never said it was the last wolf anywhere. He was told to kill a wolf and killed it. That was all.

I think this is all leading somwhere, our Wolfclaw. Even Vratchken is coming round. We are all 'of' the place but are not. The talk is leading to action and each of us needs that.

Do you know about 'wolf bullets?' I once heard a black man in Winnipeg sitting at a bar on Portage Avenue. Mid-February, dark sludge and piss-coloured snow blowing everywhere.

'Wolf bullets' he muttered.

'Wolf bullets?'

'Yeah. Remember that boy in the story who kept crying "wolf" and nobody came and he was eaten up?'

'Sure.'

'Well, wolf bullets are when you cry wolf just to get people, frightened, stirred up, riled, to your survival or advantage. You feed them wolf bullets to see where you stand. You know who your friends are then. Black folks survived hundreds of years by firing wolf bullets at white people, slave *owners and such. Protective bullets to produce a premature reaction so you can guess what the real reaction is likely to be – and take precautions.*

Wolf bullets. Some of these bullets are striking the target. When action starts, the wolf is the reference point, the Pole Star, the touchstone.

I watched the moon slip through the dark clouds and run for the open sky. The hail battered the window like bullets – wolf bullets I reckoned.

Chapter four
CONGER

John Mackenzie, said *we're off to the lobsters*. Mary replied. *Right, John but just you mind the boy.*

What is the boat , da?

Assault craft son, ideal for the lobsters. Light on the waves, low to the water for easy lifting and piling of the creels, but skittery son, keep your life jacket on.

So, Donald, just you sit tight and watch what I do.

Leeward to the small island, out onto the soft green. The boy saw the great curve of the sparkling granite mountain. Low humps of the scattered uninhabited islands beyond them in the grey dab of the Hebrides.

He saw his dad grab each float and begin pulling each creel aboard. Scuttling velvet crabs, like hairy green dancing coins, muted brown crabs like flat stones, prawns, pink as sunset. Whelks squat on stones and sea wrack. And the prize: the blueblack metal of the lobster; usually one to the creel, if two, often one claw missing. These the old man lifted tenderly, slipping thick rubber bands over the claws, easing them into a wooden fish box divided into compartments.

The boy handed the cold rubber bands or passed the salt mackerel bait for re-baiting the creels.

Wrasse like square wet rainbows, teeth like a horse's. Slithering octopus, ling, hake, haddies, cod.

The old man reached over for one of the last creels. He raised it up to the edge of the boat, something large exploding from the creel in a horrible arc. The boy saw the fat conger coming and instinctively made a small fist, punching the creature on the head. It splashed over the edge and disappeared, green into green.

His old man's eyes were wide in his head.

Jesus Christ son are you all right?
Da what was that?
A conger, son, a conger.

And thus Donald John Mackenzie became plain Conger; to complete the circle, his father and mother became Conger too.

The island had a ruined school, monastical ruins and one house. Conger's family had actually inherited the island a century before and were the last family living on it, under intense pressure from fishing interests, conservation bodies and private landlords. John Mackenzie was once offered half a million pounds for the island but refused to sell. Conger Mackenzie was the last person born on the island at a time when everybody went to Inverness. His father fished lobsters, prawns and crabs in season, and grew subsistence vegetables on the island.

The island was only fifteen minutes by outboard from the mainland but it was possible to be marooned for days at a time by storms and wind. A generator provided electricity for the house. Conger knew everything about his small island, from its wicked steep north face to the gentler leeward stone beaches where he collected quartz, cornelian, moss agates and green Iona stone. In 1901 there were thirty-three persons living on the island, fishing mostly, now there were only three.

Conger left the island as often as he wanted to. He went to primary school in Macqueensport where he stayed with his aunt; stayed at an east coast hostel during secondary school, two years in Belfast at the height of the Troubles, a spell in Glasgow.

When Conger Mackenzie came back to the island he vowed not to leave again and like his father, became obsessed with keeping the island. It would not be easy.

The man with briefcase seemed friendly enough.

'Donald John, it would be a good time to sell. Your parents are getting older and might require medical attention and care. Power cuts and gales make that more uncertain as they get older ... '

The island is not for sale.

Briefcase: 'It may not be a matter of choice, there are also conservation needs.'

The stormy petrels and puffins are safe under my care. My father, mother and I look out for nesting birds and take care of them. We keep the rats at bay and tend the ground around the ruins so people can find them who come ashore. We don't mind visitors to the island and assist them in every way possible.

'How about public access?'

It's always here.

'Think what you could do with £750,000.'

I think often of it. (He laughed thinking of it. The three of them in jeans and wellies; the old man's oilskins greased to a sheen, his mother in her favourite duster, staying in some posh hotel in Edinburgh. Beverly Fuckin Hillbillies, the old man drying haddies on the chandeliers.) He did worry about his mother but she could often stay with her sister in the town. The two men helped in every way they could around the house. His mother Mary was as attached to the island as they were.

Land and sea.

Rats were a helluva problem, rustling under the beach. They had to make special drains to keep them out of the house. Several pet cats helped, but the cats had to be kept away from nesting birds. Conger reckoned the rats would have destroyed the birds without their constant intervention. Owls, stoats and buzzards helped control the rats and troublesome rabbits but could not have kept the numbers down.

Conger argued their case with the bird people too.

Man, I know all the birds here, when they come and go. Ravens, peregrines, hoodies, eider ducks, red-headed mergansers, black guillemots, cormorants, stormy petrels, skylarks, stonechats …

The man left.

They grew trees: rowans, birches, elders, hazels and even a circle of oak which grew by the old monastery.

The sea kept the living going: crabs, prawns, lobsters, spiny lobsters, velvet crabs and whelks. Haddock and other fish were kept or given away in season.

•　•　•　•　•　•　•　•　•　•　•　•　•　•　•　•　•　•

Lights flickered in the wind, over a table of three. Rabbit stew, spuds from the garden.

'Is this what you want, Donald?' (His mother never called him Conger.)

'Yes I want to stay here. I would only sell if you wanted me to for your own health.'

John spoke. 'Remember, I feel that way about every inch of this 421 acres. But you don't have to feel that way. You've been to Belfast, Glasgow, other places. Maybe there is no future for a young man on this island, or for a wife and children. A young woman would not feel the same as we do about the place … the wind, the cold, the rats.'

'I want to remain here exactly because I've seen other places. I can fish, do this and that.'

His mother went to the stove for a pot of stew, ladling more onto each plate.

The island then is yours but it is your free will too.

He chewed the meat silently.

His mother knew *that* part of it was never easy around Macqueensport. Most young girls left for college or university and never returned from London, Edinburgh or Glasgow. He couldn't tell the old folks sex was never the difficult thing. He remembered a summer six years ago when he bedded a prodigious number of Swedish and Dutch student backpackers. Lost count in fact. A cliché. Local Hieland fishermen, a bit like the Greek/Spanish waiter motif.

Conger tried to imagine a son or daughter growing up on the island as he had done. He had his doubts and he knew his parents had too. They never had much choice in the matter. He would be the first of several generations to actually have a choice and that made it doubly difficult. He also knew his parents worried about him being left alone there. His mother would not imagine a young woman enduring what she had done, yet hoped it would be possible.

There were other concerns tied to that: to keep the rats from winning, to keep the birds returning, to keep erosion at bay and to prevent the broadleaf trees from blowing into the sea. And the sea. He had seen it in his father's creels: fewer prawns and lobsters and many undersized. More velvets and spinies, fewer big fish, more starfish. The small boat having to go further and further from shore where it was less suited to its work. He and the old man knew the real source of the problem. The big east coast trawlers coming in between the cliff and the island, disturbing the fine balance between shellfish and their natural food. But worse, the huge eastern bloc 'klondykers' moored off the island. After a storm, they saw the rocks covered in fish oil and fuel, glistening like filthy rainbows in the sun; and worse, plastic bin bags, glass bottles, fish packaging tins, old packets and buckets, used condoms (there were no women on board). They both felt the rich nutrients scorched the bottom of the sea. Their own attitudes were in the face of political correctness which portrayed idyllic relations between the fishing communities and their eastern-bloc brethren, much of which was true but the lasting pollution from the boats was a fact, not to be glossed over by school campaigns to rid the beaches of unsightly rubbish while those thriving on the trade did nothing. Conger saw the tiny primary pupils in the wind and rain, filling bin bags full of the crap washed up. The visible stuff. God knows what the invisible stuff was doing to the seabeds, where Conger's own quarry lived.

'There is no evidence of that man,' they replied every year but all the local fishermen knew things would get worse until fishing ceased altogether.

Every lobster his father caught was measured carefully with callipers and those undersize were always put back into the sea. John often put back ripe females as well, which no other fishermen did. Nor would his father sell crabs just for the fleshy 'toes'. *All the beast or nothing he would say. How would you like your arms removed?*

So, land and sea and the raised beach between them.

Cree Dan has something, Conger thought. The idea to get a group of people doing things, maybe just symbolic things. What was the Gaelic proverb? 'It's all the bigger for that, said the wren, as he pissed into the ocean.' Pissing into the ocean. He and the old man had done that plenty of times off the boat, watching the delicate warm piss curve and hit the cold sea. *All the better for that.* Thirty-five years old, halfway home and even great changes in his own lifetime. Sea trout used to leap by the thousands around the island. A boy could cast out a spinner and reel in a three pounder no bother. Salmon were common, as were the seals and porpoises feeding on them. No Russian or Bulgarian factory ships and everybody fished inshore with creels for shellfish. Now everyone except him trawled for prawns, even though trawled prawns fetched much lower prices than creeled ones, which could be shipped alive to Paris or New York. Trawled prawns arrived at the surface dead, crushed, the flesh already damaged.

Good old days.

Cree Dan was a queer bugger, anyway, some kind of half-breed medicine man whose old man was also a daft wandering bugger, never satisfied with anything. Even when he went to Canada he couldn't settle – always a kind of hobo, my old man said.

Wolfclaw: A right laugh, aye. Ivan, a big Russian nut

case. Killybegs, lazy pisshead dreamer. Vratchken. Lord have mercy. Conger thought of her black curls bouncing on the wind, her long legs wrapped in tight jeans. I've been on this island too long, he laughed in the face of the wind.

So, Wolfclaw, if I have any concerns they are only of land and sea, which is of course, everything.

Bring back the sea trout. Where have they gone?

Bring back the salmon.

Get rid of rats (including the human kind).

Bring back the lobster, crab and prawn.

Keep human beings on the island.

Cree Dan talked about 'spirit protectors' once. Let me have *two*. The adder. Where have all the adders gone? I have drunk with adders from deep mountain pools, shared a warm boulder with them under the February sun. I've seen them swimming under waterfalls. I once counted a hundred in an hour along the shores of the Red Loch. Maybe they are going the way of the wolf.

My other spirit protector. The charr. The red trout. Red belly. Tar-ruachan. There is no lovelier Highland creature. Communal fish, deep dweller, tribal fish relict of the great Ice Age. Lives so deep anglers never catch them, rarely see them. The gentle pinks and reds of them rise up from deep pools like subconscious memories. Exquisite fish, Highland survivor. No longer in the deep pools I caught them in as a kid. But where? Where? Wolfclaw, let my spirit helpers be the adder of the land and the charr of the water, before they vanish like the wolf. If they vanish, then I too vanish. Like them I am a native species – under threat.

Chapter five
KILLYBEGS

Darra Fillan, alias Killybegs. I see it sometimes, this bare land turned on its head, welded to Donegal, everything matching, Siamese twins of heather, granite, bare rock headlands. It was joined once, of course then cut loose, floating away. Siamese twins, sharing a few major organs but definitely sharing a soul. Scotland welded to Ireland again. I've done my bit. I married a local girl and have two children in the local primary school. I work as a tree planter and gardener with my brother-in-law, planting broadleaf trees throughout the Highlands.

Killybegs. I always looked across the sea to other land, landward beyond Drumanoo, Fintragh Bay and Donegal Bay to Sligo or the green slopes of Mayo. Even my father, a Mayo man, forever looked to the sea, despite him often reciting:

> *Now that summer is coming, now that summer*
> *is coming,*
> *I will cut a blackthorn stick for my hand,*
> *And I will quit this loud town for the silence*
> *of the County Mayo*
> *And in that lake-dotted, heather-scented land,*
> *This old pain will go …*
> *The rustle of the rowan tree …*

Why, Da, *the* County Mayo: What *other* Mayo is there?

Only the **sweet** County Mayo he would say, only the **sweet** County Mayo.

Scotland *and* Ireland.

My uncle would take a bus on any afternoon from the Gorbals all the way to Donegal Town. And he would sometimes take me back to Glasgow.

That bhoys. The Celtic. Dalglish and Lennox.

The grey cold terraces of the 'Jungle' at Parkhead. I could see very little of the match, only the swaying of the green and white. I sang:

> *Roamin in the gloamin*
> *by the bonnie banks o Clyde.*
> *Roamin in the gloamin*
> *with Saint Patrick by my side.*
> *When the sun is sinkin west*
> *that's the time that I love best.*
> *Oh, it's great to be a Roamin Catholic!*

The thick pie grease, lining the back of the mouth and the hot tea melting the grease, it sliding down in choking lumps and the crowd swaying and shouting:

Kenny ... Kenneeeee ... Kenneeee ... Kenneeeee ...
Scotland *and* Ireland.

And walking back through Bridgeton, Celtic scarves tucked under the jackets but:

Fenian Bastard, Kafflik Bastard, Tim, Dan, Taig.

I heard those words for the first time and my uncle said *keep walkin son, keep walkin son.* I from Killybegs, up from Dunkineely, sheltered by Slieve League, and this in Bridgeton – the colour of a cigarette stub crushed on grey sleet.

I did a gardening course in Dublin and gardened everywhere. Dublin, London, Chicago. The wandering Irishman. I swept shit off the floors of the Greyhound Bus Station in Chicago, staying with my aunt on the edge of the southside ghetto.

I admit a penchant for oak trees. I was named for one, after all. I planted acorns around the world. Why do people ever come home to Ireland? Death mainly. To bury or be buried. I've seen it all my life. Da's death brought me home. I was one of the 'six'. His saying. 'One of the *six*. You only need six men to carry your coffin at the end of the day.

You only have to make six friends in your life.'

He could have had six hundred people carry his coffin but he went down into the ground of Donegal on a slight rise, at his request, in order to 'have a view' over to Mayo. His own last wishes. 'And I will quit this loud town for the silence of *sweet Mayo.*' The *sweet* Mayo.

Meanwhile, I went trawling with Uncle Muirisheen and ended up in Macqueensport with Bulgarians, Rumanians, Russians, Latvians. I was a shite fishermen – we all knew it. Not lazy, just tired. Just a fey landsman. Muirisheen was blunt, like any Donegalman.

'*You're absolute feckin shite, Darra. As a fisherman, you're a helluva good tree planter.*' He handed me some money.

'Two thousand pounds here uncle.'

'*Your fair share of the fishing, son.*'

I looked beyond the village.

'Muirisheen, no trees here. It could be Donegal's twin.'

'*Except for religion, you're right. You'd almost think you were home in Killybegs.*'

'Maybe I am home,' I said.

I walked down the long pier in the October rain. The waves were churning. I looked beyond the white blade of the village to the hills beyond. The bracken was turning to rust, a bleeding stigmata down the bare hillside.

I stayed in a Bed and Breakfast for a few weeks, planning my next move. The next move wasn't mine.

•   •   •   •   •   •   •   •   •   •   •   •   •   •   •   •   •   •

I met Rowena Macmillan at a pub where she worked as a barmaid.

Pint of export please.

The barmaid was short and red-haired; no freckles, eyes bright shining brown, like wet chestnuts. Well-proportioned trunk and branches. She was dressed in flowers – skirt and blouse.

> *Here's your pint. You're not from around here.*
> *That's true.*
> *Are you Irish?*
> *I am.*
> *Do you have Irish?*
> *Some – I do.*
> *Do you speak Gaelic?*
> Tha.
> Pionta, mas e do thoil e.
> *A pint coming .*
> Ta an la go dona.
> Fuar agus fliuch.

So we stuck to this for a while, guessing and filling in the gaps.

> *I worked on my uncle's trawler, there by the pier, but I'm not really a fisherman. I'm a landscape gardener. I've worked in Dublin, Glasgow, Chicago. I came back for my father's funeral in Donegal.*
> *I'm sorry. Will you stay here?*
> *Yes, if I can.*
> *My brother Robert runs a tree and plant nursery. He too has worked all over the world. He studied at the Royal Botanics in Edinburgh.*

That was that. Robert Macmillan needed help. We were up early, up the coast to the big estates, private gardens and forestry properties. Like me, he preferred the broadleaves. Unlike me, he was dour.

I stayed in an extension to Robert's house and quietly kept out his way. One day in May I saw Rowena Macmillan walking along the shore. It was early evening, the light still soft, the hills now spilling with green. She was in lilac. The wind rippled her skirt and parted her long hair. This gardener was in love – seed time in the fields of Venus.

We got married and to please Rowena's parents agreed to raise the kids good Scots Protestants. I could care less. I remembered King Kenny was a Protestant but the whole of 'the Jungle' at Parkhead chanting his name. I gave a lovely potpourri to Rowena's mum in direct contradiction to her father's wish that there would never be 'popery' in his house. My own wee joke.

Two children now; Hazel five and Holly three. We live above Macqueensport in an old two-up, two-down which once belonged to an old aunt of Rowena's. My life is good. Darra Fillan. My hands are in the dirt where they belong and I am improving the garden around the house which could easily be in Donegal, for all the surrounding landscape. Robert is fine to work for; he has begun to share my passion for oak trees and we plant them wherever and whenever we can.

•   •   •   •   •   •   •   •   •   •   •   •   •   •   •   •   •   •   •   •

The girls come into the gardening shed.
Let me tell you this dream I say.
Dad, where is my ball?
Haze, I don't know. Can I finish this dream?
Dad, I want a story. Where is my ball?
It is away in Killybegs.
What is that?
Across the Ocean.
Which Ocean?
The *Irish* Ocean. The sea, the sea, *mo ghradh,
      mo chridh,* long may it flow between
      England and me.
Tell me a story.
Will a dream do?
Is it a story-dream?
It is a dream-story.
OK.

Johnny Chapman lived in America a long time ago. He worked as a blacksmith but got kicked in the head. They thought he would die but he finally recovered. He woke up and told them about his dream. He saw millions and millions of apple trees in the American wilderness. Apple trees in leaf, in white and pink blossom, in fruits of red and green, yellow and gold. The apple trees grew in one giant orchard from the Appalachian Mountains to the Mississippi. So he took a bag of apple seeds. He used his cooking pot for a hat. He wandered through the wilderness planting apple trees and building small fences around them to protect them. He never killed any living creature and made friends with all the Indians, who left him alone, thinking he was mad, crazy.

Did his dream come true? Did he plant those trees?

His dream did come true. I've seen the descendants of those trees growing along muddy rivers and corn fields, all over the Midwest, 'from old Ashtabula to frontier Fort Wayne'.

But Dad, that was *his* dream, you said you would tell us *your* dream.

Well, *my* dream is something like that. Before Holly was born, I had this dream that all the bare hills of Donegal and the Highlands were covered in mighty oak trees. All the waste fields of bracken and bare rock were covered in strong oak trees. The sheep could not kill them nor could the deer eat them or strip their bark. They grew in thick groves and in my dream, all the animals came to the oak groves to shelter from the wind and rain.

That is a strange dream. Could it ever be true?

Maybe, Hazel, it could be, then you would have to call me Darra Oak Seed or Darra Acorn. I could wander with a cooking pot on my head for a hat, from Cape Wrath to Glen Coe and up the Great Glen, planting acorns, shielding each tree with a tiny fence.

Could we all come along?

Of course. Aren't we all trees? Oak, Rowan, Hazel and Holly – all native Highland trees?

Oak. Darroch, darra, durr, derry. Hey derry down.

When Hazel found her ball and left, I thought of that greatest link between Scotland and Ireland: the oaken boats of the saints. Columba himself built a chapel of oak on Iona made from his boat.

I thought of the greatest gift of wood: my own fiddle, the jigs and reels from the static dead wood.

I met Cree Dan a few days later. Rowena told me everybody considered Dan's family strange, eccentric; harmless but weird.

But I like the man. He's canny, good crack. We talk in Gaelic up to a point. He hates my mandolin playing but I don't think he's ever heard my fiddle. The Wolfclaw is maybe nothing but good crack, a talking shop, where I can indulge my oak dreams, harmless as they are. I suppose I could welcome wolves into my oak groves. I never imagined them there. Spiders, butterflies, deer, bats, woodcocks, badgers, even wild boar.

Cree Dan and I talked once, he in Gaelic, I in Irish.

You married Rowena Macmillan?

I certainly did.

Most people don't agree with this, but I think 'Macmillan' as a surname comes from *Mac-gill-Fhaolain*, the son of the descendant of the servant of *Faolan*, the wolf saint.

I replied that I didn't know that.

But Cree Dan missed another point here. He didn't catch my own surname, 'Fillan' from Faolan, 'little wolf'.

I'll tell him that one day.

Right now, the dream is enough. In the wind and hail of a bare country on the world's edge, it is enough to *imagine* trees where there is only cold dead rock.

Chapter six
IVAN, AS TOLD BY A FRIEND

'Dozhd da dozhd' – *rain and more rain, trouble, and more trouble,* as they say in Russian. I am a friend of Ivan's. I am Russian but Ivan is from the Chuvash. I worked with him and his brother Shavly.

One spring, a few years ago, big Shavly went down to the Chuvash and waved his money around – money earned from working on the mackerel ships. Shavly impressed his sisters, but most of all, he impressed younger brother Ivan. Ivan was married with a daughter, Sura. Now, when Shavly talked, people listened. Shavly had travelled all over the world. He worked on the big ice breakers between Murmansk and Dudinka, and had been to the Canadian Arctic on a big ice breaker. Anyway, Ivan finished the spring ploughing and went with Shavly up to Murmansk, where Ivan the landsman began to learn about fish and boats. On our first journey to Macqueensport Ivan was seasick for seven days and begged us to throw him overboard. Shavly laughed and cradled his brother like a baby. Ivan was homesick too, forever taking photos of his wife Anish and daughter from his leather wallet. There was a language barrier too. Shavly spoke some Russian as did all the crew, but Ivan spoke very little, preferring to be silent or to speak his own Chuvash tongue to Shavly. But Ivan was not unpopular. He worked hard and could gut mackerel quicker than any of us except Shavly. Ivan could also sing, though none of us knew the meaning of his words.

I (my name is not important) have an eye and ear for the Ivans of the world. This life in a factory ship is both good and not good. Our life at home was not good either. The life here is cat shit and the life back there was dog shit. Different kinds of shit but they both stink. We play cards, work, wank and sleep.

• • • • • • • • • • • • • • • • • •

There was a poet named Mikhail in my District. He died in the Great Famine of 1922. Millions of people died in that hunger. All of us knew his poems by heart, poems full of beauty and dread. My father knew him but I have only seen pictures of Mikhail. Somehow, Ivan reminds me of him. One day, we were smoking that good strong Chuvash tobacco called makhora. The sky was everywhere blue and we waved to children playing on the sand. They laughed and waved back. We saw porpoises, whales, otters. Ivan began to talk in poor Russian. He talked in images.

> *This mountain is an upturned boat,*
> *purple on a sea of pink.*
> *Grey rocks moving – they are crows!*
> *Seal shakes silver threads.*
> *Mountains with teeth of ice.*
> *Sea gulls are winged puppets.*

Ivan had never spoken to me before. He was to speak to me often in Russian after that. He said he was sorry but he did not like Russians nor did he like the police or the Russian state. He talked about simple things – about his life on the land; growing makhora, hemp, flax, sugar beet, wheat, barley and buckwheat. Ivan began to make sketches—of boats, the shore line, the mountains, the village, the birds. Mainly, he sketched the bare land.

His manner was changing. He was working hard, filleting mackerel and herring, putting them into our flat tins. He was never up on deck but always down in the stinking factory, head down, silent. Shavly wasn't his usual self which was laughing , swearing (no one could swear like Shavly) telling filthy jokes, boosting morale, slapping backs, passing out cigarettes. Shavly, shifting between languages, singing, arguing, translating, maybe Ivan's direct opposite.

He dark, Ivan blond, he laughing, Ivan silent, sketching and writing, in Chuvash.

Dozhd da dozhd. Ivan's silence was one way of dealing with our life on board.

Fate, alcoholism, prison, death, police, fate, fate, fate. The *Russian* story, the *Russian* blues.

Woke up this mornin,
KGB knockin at my door.
Woke up this mornin,
broken vodka bottles on the floor.
Woke up this mornin
in the hard guts of booze,
snow blockin my front door,
I got the Russian blues.

Cat shit, dog shit, they both stink. 'They' watch our every move when we go ashore, when we slice the mackerel, when we piss overboard, when we take our pay. Those like Shavly soar above it all but get crushed in the end. 'Freedom' is a word they use in the West. It is an alien concept to us Russians, where fate is fate. But those of the Chuvash our different. They have many words for freedom in their language.

Then bad weather came. Bad fishing followed and we had nothing to do. Our ship was ordered to leave and we knew we would probably never be coming back. This was the worst of a string of bad seasons. The ship would require expensive maintenance and would probably be scrapped. We would have to find other work.

The storm came and our huge steel factory whose name means 'Steadfast' broke her moorings and floated like one of our mackerel tins. It nearly turned over, spilling tins and shelves. The factory floor filled up with mud, grease and fish oil and we could do nothing as our ship wedged between the rocks off the edge of the island whose cliff face we knew so well. Then a miracle, the Scottish wind shifted and we were blown free with as much force as had blown us in. Chaos, confusion, shouting, swearing but the ship rode out to the open sea where the wind seemed less. Having already officially quit the port, we continued for home. There was much damage and loss to our machinery and factory but the ship was seaworthy – at least enough to get home.

There was one loss that could never be made good. On the second night when we all sheltered safely in our bunks, big Ivan disappeared.

'He was washed overboard and drowned,' said Shavly.

All that was really left of Ivan was an empty bunk and full foot locker. Shavly kept the sketch books. We searched for two days but no body was found and the weather worsened. Finally, we were forced to leave the search to the Scottish authorities. We went home. Ivan the planter of barley, thus was himself planted in the deep Scottish sea.

The ship was scrapped in Murmansk and we all went back where we had come from. I became a caretaker in a public toilet in Odessa. A different kind of shit but it all stinks. *Dozhd da dozhd.*

• • • • • • • • • • • • • • • • • • •

Ivan's story in his own words.
I did not want to stay in the Chuvash, that's why I came on the ship in the first place. My home. THEY are cutting down our trees, covering our ploughed earth with cement, killing our wolves, slaughtering our great Beluga sturgeon to extinction. THEY will come for Shavly one day. THEY will kill our language. Shavly and I argued for hours about this. I told him I would seek asylum here and bring my wife and child. This Scotland is a big land but the ground needs ploughed,

fed and nurtured. I studied the land carefully from the deck of our ship. The oak is my father, the birch is my mother, we say. Birches are plentiful, but there are no oaks here so this land is only half alive. Bare, so bare.

• • • • • • • • • • • • • • • • •

'Shavly man, I will walk into a church and stay there.'

'Like bitching fuck you will. I would be arrested. They would take our pay until you gave up. You would be a crazy scum fuck to do such a thing.'

'I will seek asylum.'

'How? Why? You are free back home. Nobody is after you.'

'THEY are all after us, after our rich country because they have destroyed their own.'

'Shit fire, younger brother, shit fire and save your safety matches. They won't let you stay here. You are *not* being persecuted at home.'

Shavly could not understand. He is fearless. Fearless men are stupid.

I was thinking, writing, sketching. But I had an idea. I hated the rubbish our men threw overboard but I saw how the prevailing winds always drove it into the rocks of the island nearest our mooring. The cliff there was steep but there was a path inland, beginning where the rubbish collected. A path into an island where it seemed nobody lived.

Shavly didn't like the idea. He said it was *a bitching scum shit of a sturgeon turd of an idea; a putrid mare's milk of a whorehouse wall scrapings idea.*

I said the idea could not fail as long as our rivers the Sura and Anish flow to the sea, which is forever for *even* the Russians would never fill our rivers with concrete.

'Don't bet against it,' hissed Shavly, his teeth shining like mackerel blades.

Ah, the idea, the storm.

Our boat shook like a child's toy in the bath, breaking its moorings. All the men were cowering in the middle factory. Shavly must have been there for I think I remember Shavly's cigarette like a beacon, and his white teeth like a living white streak against the cold dark. I lost no time, knowing the wind would drive this huge metal monster into the rocks of the island. It took me ages to get to the deck, where I crouched like an animal, waiting for the sound. The force nearly broke me in two, and wrenched my left arm out of its socket. Then came a calm, the wind died, I could see through the rain. The wrack-covered rocks came into view and without thinking, I leapt for them, nearly slipping back under the ship. The wind whirled me around and I fell. Then the wind shifted suddenly and I heard the boat crunch against the rocks before it headed for the open sea. I clung to the ground like I wanted to plant myself there. I crawled like a baby towards the glinting rubbish in a pile at the end of the rocks.

I stumbled beyond the rubbish, into the face of the shifting wind and rain and fell again onto the grass of the island. Then, I saw a fence on an island where I thought there were no people. I followed the fence, my back to the wind, my right hand gripping the fence wire. When the rain stopped, I could see some lights flicker on and off on the mainland shore. I crawled to a low stone building and pulled myself inside. It was dry. The pain in my left arm throbbed. I fell asleep.

I learned later this building was the remains of an ancient Celtic monastery. This was told to me at dawn by a powerful man with hair of many colours.

'I'm Conger,' he said. 'Who the hell are you?'

• • • • • • • • • • • • • • • • • • •

The man kept me hidden on the island. He fed and clothed

me. I learned from him that events in the Soviet Union had made my case a routine one. I was now one of many refugees. After many more months, I was granted asylum. Soon, Anish and Sura will be joining me in Scotland.

Shavly knew I did not drown the night of the storm. He knew of my plan. He even kept his mouth shut, nearly impossible for him. He is working the ice breakers again and I will miss him. But I told him he could keep my notebooks.

Dozhd da dozhd. True, but sometimes, *even* in Scotland, it stops raining.

Chapter seven
VRATCHKEN

Ay, ay, fit like? Foo's aa wi ye? Jist aye tyaavin awa? Sorry, ken. Ye divna ken i spik o i north east. Ah spik English tae, wi a bittie back-slidin, ken?

East, tae i risin sun isnae gweed, ken.

OKAY, Ah'll hae a go wi English.

Explorers, fugitives, holy men go west, *always* west. Land of Youth. Land of the Blessed Isles, westering home, west is best. I'm going where the sun will be sinking.

But east. East is effete, decadent, admission of defeat, busted clean. Think of every country's west: excitement, mountains, clear rivers, native peoples. Canada, America, Australia, Scotland, Ireland. Gaan west, ma loon, gaan west. Ken.

My father's family was in Macqueensport before Macqueen was a bairn and a midwife named Rowie Rowan delivered me in the bed in the upstairs room of a gabled cottage on the shore. Can't get more local than that.

Here I am back. I am a tall quine, good looking, men are always trying to feel me up and whistling at me. Aye, I am dark and comely and maybe there will be time for all that. I have good breasts, long legs, fine teeth and black curly hair that some daft poet-mannie frae Foggie once said looked like *oil-slicked sea wrack*. There you go.

My life is a geography. It is in my speech. From the west: treeless, bracken, gorse, broom, snowmelt creaming off the hills, stags and hinds twitching on the horizon, lone buzzards keekin roon i cloods :

Mo shoraidh leis ... soraidh leis ... Tha mi a'dol ...

To a brooch, that place where Gaelic floats from the west and Scots from the east, the straths have widened, the ground is more fertile, trees, now – beech and oak, flood plain wider, the towns have shrubs and hanging baskets. All of it now shading east:

buildings of a different stone, chips giving way to stovies, farms climbing up the horizon, wind-bevelled trees. 'Backhill', 'Loanhill', stirkies, myaavs, peesies, aathin clarty an caul, roch an raxin. East.

Vratchken MacIntyre.

My parents sent me east because I knew how my mother was getting those black eyes. I was the oldest of six and would have told. I think I was a sacrificial lamb, to keep the family peace. At ten, I was sent to my Aunt Agnes (my mother's sister) and Uncle Charlie, decent old-fashioned folk with no children of their own. Charlie hurt his back on the farm – he was 'the barley king' – and some settlement money let them buy a big guest house. It was not a grand house for rich folks but just a big house rescued from dereliction. The house was three miles from the town and school, down a long single track of gorse, near fields in barley or hay, or stubble; spring wheat or oats. Pheasants ran in front of you, down the narrow road which ended with the house. A path then picked up from the road, winding through the forest to the river and footbridge.

I never counted the rooms but my first thought was: *this is the Cluedo house*. Library, lounge, dining room, study, big kitchen, tall ceilings with chandeliers.

My room was my world. Bed, dresser, desk. I could stand on my tiptoes and see the tops of the chestnut tree, summer and winter. I would lay back in bed watching the stars in the picture frame of the window, the picture changing with the seasons. In winter, buzzards perched on the highest branches. Doves and blackbirds woke me up in the morning.

My chores were few, even at the height of the tourist season. I took bacon and toast to the guests; in colder weather, I brought in wood and coal for the fires; mainly just for the lounge and dining room. My aunt and uncle never had children of their own. They were kind and gave me more attention and freedom than I would have at home. My Aunt Agnes called me 'Vratchken' as a joke, because I was the most *vratchless* child they could imagine. I liked peace and quiet and always tried to find the way to find it.

I stayed there from the age of ten, until I left the Academy at seventeen. I did visit home. Ma shuffled about like a hurt, wounded animal and could never really look me in the eyes. Maybe because I looked just like her, maybe she felt she should have fought to keep me at home. Da was never there. I suppose he was in the pub. That's *it*. A futret. Ma looked like a futret.

Christmas in the big house was a special time. Charlie and Agnes had a huge pine tree put in the library. Its top reached the tall ceiling. They always had a fire going and when they put the lights off, the lights from the tree bounced off the chandelier and caught the light from the dancing fire and the effect was that of a lovely tree-woman dancing with her dark shadow. I sat for hours in the room, in the dark, putting logs on the fire, listening to the rain and hail outside on the big windows, wrapped in the warm safety of all this. I could keek through the curtains behind the tree and watch the fields fill with deep snow.

My brothers and sisters came to visit sometimes but I'm sure they never felt the magic of the place, but dad and mum never came to the house. I would greet in my room at night, wondering at my strange exile in a big house with two old people who clearly loved me more than my parents; I'd marvel at my head of hair, seen in the adjoining mirror, like an oil spill on my clean pillow but my tears were mostly tears of happiness.

The fields were a logical extension of the house. The front garden was bounded by a wall at the far end, with borders of shrubs, herbs and flowers along all three walls. The river lay a mile beyond the far wall, with a marshy meadow in between. In spate, the river yielded sea trout and salmon. Beyond the river, hills rose up, topped by scattered hill farms, like an amphitheatre with seats of changing colours; variously green, black and brown. Two sides of the house were a tangle of narrow roads leading to other and farms but east of the house was the real frontier, deep forests with paths leading to the river – paths used by poachers and walkers mostly, there not being enough access for anglers.

I learned the trees first. Blackthorn, rowan, hazel, elder, older beeches and oaks; planted but ancient, yews, chestnuts and monkey puzzles, planted when the house was young. Birds looped in and out of the trees: doves, owls, buzzards, hoodies and rooks, and all the smaller songbirds. Peesies were common over the fields. The fields were mostly cut for hay, the stubble attracting pheasants and rabbits, which in turn attracted foxes, badgers, stoats, weasels and wildcats.

My contempt for da took away all fear. I thought this way. Da wanted us to fear him. I didn't fear him. Contempt is not the same as fear. Contempt is *stronger* than fear. Therefore, I will have contempt instead of fear. Not contempt for everything though. Da never hit me, only my mum, but I remember his grey face growing darker and his fist would swoop down like a bird – down and across. He left, door slamming, ma like some crumpled rabbit who had just been spared by a hawk – spared, and no more. She ran to the bathroom and locked herself in, cooling the bruises I think.

No, the dark woods had no fear for me, who knew every hiding place there, and every tree that could be climbed. Freedom, on the edge of fear, but contained and woven, like a fleecy jumper keeping in the warmth. School was OK but I didn't make any real close friends, though could have. They made fun of me a little, at first, with my broad 'a's' and the way I would say 'that boys', 'that stairs', 'that teachers'. I was good at sports, especially netball, and that helped. Later, I was star of the swimming team, and was the leading pupil in languages. I got my highers and stayed on for sixth year. I knew too that I didn't want to go to University in Aberdeen, not yet anyway. I wanted my freedom but learned to fillet haddies instead.

• • • • • • • • • • • • • • • • • •

Stevie's Seafoods. I had a white boiler suit with thermal wellies, gloves and showercap hat. I had a sharp knife that could fillet a haddie in seconds with two cuts. *Vratchken, Ali Baba o i fisher quines, min thi fillum wi Ali slicing yon Turkmannies?* I worked in a trance, numb from the cold but good at something and the quinies treated me like one of them, though often wondering aloud why I didn't have a fella yet. Maybe all this was a puzzle to Charlie and Agnes but they never said and I paid them for my board now, but it was the fish that *grew* me; knowing haddies and cod, getting into the office and later to college where I learned four languages so I could do business with the eastern-bloc ships. Then the job took me to Macqueensport where I rented a cottage of my own, just up the braes. I often visited ma and my brothers and sisters. I just as often saw dad staggering down the shore, shaking his fist at the stars.

• • • • • • • • • • • • • • • • • •

I missed the big house and its Christmas tree and the soft snow on its slates and on the boughs of the bonny chestnut, green and rippling above my soft white room. Once I read the Russians, Turgenev, Tolstoy and Chekhov, and realized my house was like a Russian summer house, amid hay and grain, with a slow river in the background, where pre-Revolution families played garden games, eating and drinking under the sun and stars. I always thought Vratchken sounded Russian, though I kent ah wasnae a vratch, ken, ivver, ken.

• • • • • • • • • • • • • • • • • •

One more thing though. One New Year, when I was twelve, it was a crisp frosty morning and I went out to gather some kindlers for the big living room fireplace. I remember the sun glinting off the hard frost. I gathered some sticks and put them in the wooden box in the wood shed. I decided to walk a bit further, because I had never seen tree branches coated in ice before. I walked towards the forest, along the row of beeches, shining in their icy shellac. Then, I saw it, beyond the chestnut tree. It was a black panther, a big cat, stalking a pheasant which had just scurried into view. The huge beast exploded forward, and ran into the forest with the bright pheasant fluttering in its jaws.

My heart was pounding but the feeling was more exhilaration than fright. I thought how often I'd gone to those woods on my own, climbing trees, gathering conkers or kindlers. Charlie and Agnes must have never seen the beast or they would never have let me go to the woods alone. I sucked in the cold air and took the box of sticks into the house. I helped Aunt Agnes with the chores, peeling spuds, preparing the sprouts, gathering leeks from the walled garden but all through tea, I sat in a kind of delicious trance, with a great private knowledge that something forbidden and impossible could be known to me alone and that I had been 'chosen' to see it.

I climbed up to my room that night and stared from the window into the dark. I shivered with a strange tingle, thinking of the sleekness and power of what I'd seen and what other things the New Year might bring.

The next day, I had my first period.

And I never saw that black beast again, though I looked for it often enough.

Chapter eight
CREE DAN

We next met in early December. It had been a bright day. The sky was blue, sea calm and the fishing, good; the big Klondykers were readying themselves for a journey home during the break for Christmas when all the big north-east trawlers went home until the New Year. The Haddock Arms was busier too, both during the day and evening and the impending holiday cheered the place up. I thought our room looked a bit brighter than usual. We sat around the table, while a good fire roared in the grate, everybody gradually shedding their outdoor hats, scarves and coats.

Killybegs lost no time. 'You're the Alpha Wolf, man, start howlin.'

'OK. The Wolfclaw is a combination of the Boy Scouts, the Girl Guides, the Fianna, the A Team, the Merry Pranksters, The Vigilantes and the Scottish Women's Rural Institute.'

'Wi a *difference*, ken.' Vratchken put her orange juice down and brushed her wet hair back. 'With a *difference*. We're aa the same in a way. Here and no here, there and no there. We've all been away, so we have a grounds for comparison. Question though, Dan, this is like the bluidy UN here. Which language do we use?'

'Well, I've got English, Gaelic, Cree and some Assiniboine but English is the strongest.'

We went round the table.

'I have the Chuvash, Russian and English in that order.'

Killybegs put forward English and Irish in *that* order.

Conger: 'Gaelic and English in equal measure, but stronger in written English.'

Vratchken offered Gaelic, English, north-east Scots, Russian, Bulgarian and Rumanian!

Vrathcken spoke to Ivan. 'Ya govoryu po-rooski, nah ne ochen horosho svoboden.'

'Ah ken,' grinned Ivan.

'We can all work this way. Every one of us has a language other than English we can communicate in. This might be handy at times. Killybegs, Conger, Vratchken and myself in Gaelic or Irish. Vratchken to Ivan in Russian. We can choose English for Ivan's sake.'

Our name was next. Everybody agreed on Wolfclaw, though Howlin Wolf and the SWRA (Scottish Wolf Restoration Association) were suggested.

Purpose? 'Vratchken, you have a go.'

She swept her dark hair back again.

'Take Macqueensport as a symbol. Co-operation, clear water, clean air, the living is good. There is really nothing wrong with the place, ken. There is no problem in society that is not reflected here; drugs, alcoholism, violence, de-population. But you've got to separate general problems from particular ones. You could argue that there is no need for a secret club or group because all these problems are being dealt with by social workers and politicians.'

Conger nodded. 'But sometimes, opinion can be moulded or hastened by the acts of a few bolder people who take the initiative.'

Killybegs interrupted by going for drinks. 'The usual. Vodka for Ivan, orange juice for Vratchken, whisky and chaser for the Gaels.'

He returned with the drinks.

'Quorum?'

'Three.'

'Voting?'

'Majority. Consensus not likely here.'

'New members?'

'Caa canny. In time, maybe.'

I offered more. 'I see us listing our problems and the purpose of the group becomes the solution of problems by agreed methods, limiting the means to our ends.'

More discussion followed. Pub business was picking up but I had young Ribalda Mackenzie on the till, backed up by Hamish Cyart, as more noise picked up from next door.

Ivan pounded the table for attention.

'In the Chuvash, we wish to feed, clothe and house everybody, taking care of the weak and the ill. We wish also to fight our oppressors, but there, the oppression is direct so we know what we are fighting against.'

'Ivan is right,' said Conger 'but do we use violence against people or property here?'

'Conger, ah ken, but if we have to break the law sometimes we don't have to use violence against people, in fact, we'll win more sympathy by being clever and creative. Humour will create more sympathy. By the way, Cree Dan, is taking minutes such a good idea when the *claw* starts scratchin, ken?'

I kent fine. I told her I would take care of that without jeopardising anyone.

Our meeting broke up just after official closing time. I opened the door to the night and heard their excited voices echoing down the moonlit street, breath puffing clouds into the winter air.

Late that night, I wrote.

NAME: Wolfclaw

MEMBERS: Five

QUORUM: Three

VOTE: Majority

MOTTO: Hic lupi abundant.

OBJECTIVE: To identify and solve problems, symbolically, with humour.

METHODS: Peaceful, non-violent (possibly

sometimes illegal) clandestine. Violence against 'property' sometimes permitted but only after full discussion.

STATEMENT: The wolf is a symbolic animal, portrayed in folklore as cunning and treacherous. It has thus been hunted and nearly exterminated all over the world. Yet, in fact, the wolf is communal, protective, loyal and lends its strengths to the group as a whole, without which the individual wolf can't survive. From its ranks came the dog, identified with courage, loyalty and sacrifice. The wolf's qualities are best understood by aboriginal peoples who shared their landscape with the wolf and maybe even modelled some of their own societal traits on its habits. Wolfclaw reflects many of those original cultures in its members, in their concern with culture and languages, for Cree, Gaelic, Irish and other languages reflect the same fate as the wolf. Each member of the Wolfclaw has particular rapport with animals and plants, of land and sea. The bringing together of these people can not be *just* luck or fortune.

We are only five people who are also known and respected in the place we live and work; a place we also care deeply for, having been connected in most ways with exile from that place, or exile to that place. What we do will probably be misunderstood and be seen as harmful. We will also do illegal things. *Action symbolique* may have grave un-symbolic consequences; witness, dumping tea in a harbour, knocking down a tyrant's statue, stealing an historic stone or artifact. Yet, somehow, these acts mobilise feelings and help focus them in a way argument or logical discussion never could. In essence:

1) Identify problems
2) Identify solutions
3) Decide on team course of action
4) All action is volunteer

• • • • • • • • • • • • • • • • • • •

After I wrote this, I had many thoughts 'off the record.' I think in three languages, like this. Pretend I am walking down a road with a dog at my side. He is a brindled dog, *Gaelic*. Soon we are joined by an *English* dog, a bulldog, say. Finally a *Cree* camp dog joins in, sinewy, nervous, low-slung like a coyote. They trot along with me, but leave the path to pursue a scent before returning. They leave at random, return at random, but all three never leave at the same time. It is also unpredictable how the three dogs will behave with one another at any given moment. However, at rare moments, the three align perfectly, in perfect harmony, then my thinking becomes almost a new sense and I see things clearly – too clearly.

•   •   •   •   •   •   •   •   •   •   •   •   •   •   •   •   •   •   •

There is a lot of bullshit about my mother's people – the First Peoples. They have been idealised as noble sons of nature, communing with spirits, making wise pronouncements. Well, my people are scattered all over the world, bloated on junk food and cheap alcohol, rustling in trash cans, puking up in Greyhound Bus Stations, passing out on library steps from Halifax to San Francisco, communing only with cracks in sidewalks and sewers. That should not be but that is the truth.

It was my father who claimed second sight in his family. A great-grandfather walked down a gorse-lined country road one summer evening, not a care in the world. He saw a funeral coming toward him. The coffin was opened for him. He recognized a man in it who was not to die for another three years.

My mother was more blunt about this.

'Native peoples live by their eyes and ears. This is basic science. This sight is no more than informed guessing, sensory overload with conclusions drawn from it. We "see" the likely outcome, then simply say what we see. No mystery, just physics. Every fact is a profound mystery. Just ask the coyote.'

My mother *did* talk to coyotes but that is another matter.

Anyway, see me, I am in my room above the Haddock Arms bar. I have a bed, an old armchair, a chest of drawers, a writing desk and two wardrobe cupboards. My view is out over the harbour but tonight, the window is glazed over with ice. I have a mirror on my wardrobe but I can only see my face in it if I get down on my knees. Face: nothing special, jet black hair plaited in two pigtails. It has been like this since the age of twelve. Medium height and weight, muscular. Not handsome, not ugly, not exceptional. I light the fire and go into my dream.

When I was about twelve years old, I saw with my eyes open a friend of mine named Tall Cougar McCarthy lying in a pool of blood, even though he was playing football at the time I saw this. In the waking dream, he was a man of about twenty-five, but he looked pretty much the same. I said nothing to him and we carried on kicking the ball. About twelve years later, Tall Cougar was shot dead in a robbery somewhere in Quebec; he was an innocent bystander.

I also thought my old man was doomed somehow and I think he knew it, as if he was just passing time until he met his fate face-to-face. Every time he left, I never expected to see him again. He had a doomed man's walk and speech. Maybe that was just a feeling. He always looked to the horizon.

I sit in my room with only the fire for light, and as the ice begins to melt from the windows, the water runs down like tears. I watch the flickering of blue flame, yellow and orange.

I see a loch clearly, the wide grey of it. I see it in the fire. There is a wide burn flowing into it, flowing out of a loch higher in the hills which is in turn connected to a series of smaller lochans, each connected with a burn. There are swans on the loch. The hills to the left are higher and snow-covered. Following the burn to the last loch, another burn comes from the snowy hills, fed by freshets higher up. Up from the last loch is a small strath, hidden from view until one is almost level with it. That burn is strangely white, probably because of the snowmelt or the white stones lining the burn itself. I will be going up that burn – for *what* I cannot say.

The suns rises over Macqueensport, the sky is pink, the sea is the colour of claret. Seagulls are squawking their rusted gates in the air and boats are coughing into life. Dreams are gone, giving way to grunts, coffee pots and cigarettes and curses over cigarette lighters which won't light.

The Haddock Arms is full of flickering embers and glasses not cleaned from the night before. Tiny mice scamper over the floor, looking for dropped crisps and peanuts, their eyes shimmering in the bright light streaming through the windows.

Dreams retreat before the dawn. There is a lot of work needing done.

Chapter nine

Dan: All of us were worried about Ivan, not least because of his knife-wielding conviction that he would never betray a group who had so far only met for a quiet drink in a shabby bar. 'The SWRI – wi balls, ken' noted Vratchken. A few days after the meeting, Ivan came in the back door, always reserved for personal visits outside business hours in the Haddock Arms.

'Dan, may I have a talk please?'

I poured strong coffee for both of us.

'My wife and daughter are coming in two weeks and I will meet them in London. I am frightened for them although I know this is for the best. My own homeland will be swallowed up finally and this is a chance.'

'Are all your papers OK?'

'Yes, Dan, I will be given a conditional admission into this country, then it should be a formality my staying after that.'

'*Conditional?*'

'I must have a job and prove I am taking proper steps to house myself and must stay clear of any criminal convictions. I must also have a sponsor – someone to sign papers for us. Conger's mother and father said they would do that.'

'Ivan, I don't have much power or status but as of tomorrow, you are the official handyman and part-time barman of the Haddock Arms and your wife and daughter can help expand this into an inn with room and board, as it was in its early days. You and I can knock down a few walls in the old staff quarters, making a good flat for all of you until you find something better.'

Ivan and I were sitting in the corner where the watery sun of an early December day slanted onto the table, onto our cooling coffee. We watched gulls wheel and turn over the fishing boats, watched seals bobbing in the water near the pier. The clouds overhead were moving quickly.

Ivan was not facing me, but I could see the sun reflecting small prisms of tears in the corner of his eyes. He gripped my hand, nearly spilling my coffee. He locked his thumb in mine.

'I will not forget this, Dan.' He was almost sobbing then. But I was trying to forget something too. Our Wolfclaw had great potential for one thing anyway – law-breaking – and Ivan and his family had the most to suffer from this and might even face deportation to a land that might be engulfed in civil war and social upheaval. Yet, Ivan's loyalty was frightening and unyielding. We would have to go easy on this, maybe keeping Ivan on the back burner until the rest of us were on surer ground. We'd already seen enough of Ivan to know he had a sixth sense – a paranoia which could strip away all subtlety and deceit. I would have to get to know the Chuvash man better.

'Right, big man, let's take a walk. It's a fine day for it.'

We downed our coffee and walked out the back door.

We walked on the pier first, watching the trawlers disappear up the loch. Forklifts and vans criss-crossed the pier like angry beetles while sea gulls picked at bits of fish in drying fishing nets. Cruise boats were being made ready for winter dry-dock while small boats were being loaded with provisions for the journey out to the big fish factory ships. Big Ivan seemed a bit nervous at some of the sailors coming ashore. 'Bulgarians,' he hissed. The pier traffic was picking up for the day ahead so we walked from the pier to the street, along the shopfronts. This time of year the people were almost all locals, who nodded at Ivan and grinned. He was popular and his defection was now public knowledge. The manner of it had entered into local folklore. I grinned at 'the Russian's Leap' as a place now on local imagined maps. Like all giant men, Ivan had no idea of other people's perceptions of him and no idea at all of his own physical presence and strength.

We sat on a bench, watching starlings peck at crisp packets.

'Do people ever *come to* Scotland? So many people leave that I don't think they will understand this. Why would a ploughman from the Chuvash come here?'

'Ivan, people in Scotland will have to get used to the idea, for people are coming back here from all over the world. I should know that, at least.'

We left the shore and walked up a steep path bounded by heather and bracken. There was an immediate change in Ivan as we left the sea for the land. He became more alert, more animated. He began to read the land as most people read a book and this was a land about which he yet knew little; none of its history or pain.

'The reeds could stay but drainage would create a pond here, slowing the erosion. A windbreak would create possibilities for an orchard and native hardwood trees. The trees would attract songbirds which would also aid the propagation of seeds. Small birds attract bigger birds which prey on rats and other vermin. I would graze pigs here to clear the land of bracken. Further drainage would be needed. Who knows, a man could plant oats and barley here, or maybe even tobacco.'

His eyes darted as he talked. His face was bright. We walked further until we could see the village and sea loch spread out before us. That day, Ivan missed nothing: every bird and plant was commented on, became part of a plan.

'This land is only a sick man, but because he has not been healthy, he accepts his illness as the norm. Eventually, the illness is seen as the only possibility and health is seen as an illness, an impossibility.'

'Ivan, the way of life here has been tied to a sad history where men here have had to survive, before all else.'

'No, Dan, I do not find fault but as a Chuvashi, I feel the land as a holy thing and this land needs nurture and care or it will die completely.'

'What would you grow here Ivan?'

'The same. Barley, oats, wheat, grass. I'd leave this all to lie fallow so the wildlife can flourish season after season. I would feed the soil. The landsmen here would know these things themselves. With all this water, I would probably attempt rice growing!'

He laughed and gripped me in a headlock, pushing me over into the bracken. He sat down on a rock and reached into a pouch for tobacco. At his back, the loch sparkled in the crisp air, the boats like bathtub toys. The mountains caught much of the light, in a jigsaw of light and dark pieces. I had this feeling again that all was right with this world, with the clean white village below. The Wolfclaw could only be a social club, a coffee klatch of misfits and malcontents, and yes, in my case, *nowhere men* neither one thing nor another, belonging nowhere, least of all here.

Ivan was rolling one of his mighty makhora cigarettes. The papers were dwarfed in his huge beefsteak hands. He laid the tobacco in long, stringy shards and finally lit the roll-up. Its aroma was pungent and tangy. He puffed a cloud out, and leaned back on the rock.

'Listen, Dan. This land is fine. Its people are good. But there is also more, always something more. See this tobacco pouch. What do you think it is made of?'

I thought of Russian mammals. Fox, mink, wolf?

'Feel it.'

I did. It felt like steel wool but also had a silky feel that was not like fur at all. I could not guess.

'Remember,' said Ivan, 'I told all of you once in the pub. I said it was made from a ... from a ... how do you say ... a woolly mammoth.'

I laughed. 'That would be expensive, to get enough fur from a mammoth frozen for centuries in a block of ice in Siberia.'

He laughed deeply, and blew further smoke rings into the air before he spoke.

'No, it was not frozen, it was living. Sit down and I will tell you how it came to be.'

I needed to sit down, and Ivan told me.

Ivan's tobacco pouch:
My own grandfather lived during the time of the Great Famine and epidemic after World War I, when thousands of peasants starved to death in Russia. In fact, there were millions who died. He said he had even heard of cannibalism. The Red Army and various political bands could hunt as units, so the people could not compete for the animals of the forest or the fish of the rivers. One day, my grandfather pulled a huge catfish from the Sura, which he hoped to hide until he could cut it up into bits and take home again to feed his family and friends but a ragged band of soldiers came out of the forest and took the huge fish from him, kicking him to the ground. He and the other older men held council and decided the best way was to form a hunting party and disappear into regions like the Taiga – the huge birch forest – where the soldiers would not likely be. The hunters would work in teams, some killing, others drying and curing the meat for return to the villages. Working in groups would provide armed protection. My grandfather was chosen along with six other men. Remember, they were starving and did not really have the strength for the trek but they also knew desperate action was needed because their women and children would all weaken and succumb to typhus and cholera. There was no law and order. They left some armed men with the villages and set off.

Ivan rolled another makhora cigarette and continued:

The Taiga was a magical place. A vast forest of conifers and birches, giving protection to wolves, bears, and even tigers and for a time, the men forgot their real task. The hunting was not that good. There seemed to be famine among the animals themselves. My grandfather thought the Taiga was becoming empty because the animals were feeding off human corpses in the villages, so they had to go deeper and deeper into the forest to find less and less game. They did kill wolves and foxes, and dry the meat for transport back but some of the meat went rank or was stolen by marauders. Two of the men froze to death and my grandfather said it took some will power simply to bury the men and not be tempted by cannibalism. The men were in a kind of dream, in a deep forest far from the worst of the famine and civil war. They inhaled the perfume of gentian, sedges, wild thyme, alpine poppy, crowfoot and orchid. My grandfather said ever afterwards the smell of thyme took him immediately back to that autumn in the Taiga. At night, the men built tents of leaves and stayed alive drinking hot teas made from the plants of the forest. They killed small birds and mice but big game stayed away. Then one day, they came across a new smell, a huge pile of spoor filled with the smell of orchids and poppy. Then they saw the tracks ... *this big* said grandfather, pointing from his elbow to his finger tips. The men were starving to death and didn't have much strength to continue, when they came into a clearing and saw a huge beast eating leaves from a tree. It was a *living* mammoth! My grandfather was delirious with fear and excitement and the men all shot at once. The mammoth bellowed and ran, crashing dead onto the forest floor. The men rushed the beast and some actually ate its flesh raw; others simply set about flensing the beast as they would a whale. They feasted on the animal for a few days, then cooked as much of the meat as they could carry. The cold weather kept the meat from spoiling and they made it back to the village after much hardship. They told the villagers it was bear meat. They swore themselves to secrecy but my father was told the story at my grandfather's deathbed and I think I am the only one who knows that the men, women and children survived that year of famine on the meat of an animal that wasn't supposed to exist. I often think that may have been the last one but even today, men don't go deep into the Taiga so who knows?

'That is a wonderful tale, Ivan, but why did you tell it to me when it is such a secret among your own people?'

'I told it to you Dan because it is what our lives will be about. Some people are allowed to see beyond what is; they can't be satisfied with the vision of others. This tobacco pouch was made from fur taken during that famine, as proof of my peoples' salvation. This tobacco pouch belonged to them; it will be given to to my eldest child as a reminder that dreams can feed you, keep you alive at the worst of times. And I hope, Dan, that you will not try to protect me from risk. It won't work you know. How can you deceive a man whose grandfather killed a mammoth?'

He was right. I wouldn't even try.

Chapter ten

Killybegs: I walked out on a morning which reminds everyone – incomer and local – why the Highlands is the most beautiful landscape on earth. The sky was a brittle blue, dappled with slashes of pink and gold. Snow flickered on the mountains where the sun and cold coated everything in a rich shellac, a high gloss that made the blues, greens and pinks almost three-dimensional against the rich whites and greys of cottages and stone walls.

I scraped the ice from my blue van's windscreen and started the engine. I drove down a stretch of moorland until I came to a forestry track leading through conifers so thick that the sun was blotted out. I saw what I hoped to see: Vratch's red Volkswagen Polo.

'Fit like, Killy?'

'A grand day, fine, Wolf sister but is it too cold for the task at hand?'

'Na, na, the soil will warm up soon.'

'Is this insane, Vratch, I mean, will this make any difference?'

'Isnae insane, wi Christmas comin and aa. Do you have the tools?'

I held up the two logging saws, the sun striking prisms from their cold blades. 'These will cut through anything. I had the blades specially made. Only been used twice.'

Both our cars were parked off the road, camouflaged by fallen timber. We walked on the hard snow to a gorge, then into a more open meadow, finally crossing a deer fence into a smaller plantation which could only be viewed from the high forested hill above or from a helicopter. Even then the trees were so thickly planted that gaps would not easily be seen.

And Vratchken and I were making gaps, in the broad swathe of Lodgepole pine and Sitka spruce.

'Fine trees, ken' said Vratch, barely looking up, sawing continuously.

'Finer in Alaska or Colorado though – skip a few trees so big gaps don't appear. Watch these damn prickly Sitka Spruce.'

We cut long into the morning, until the sun was nearly overhead. I paused to watch jets going to America or Africa, leaving white vapour trails in the sky like livid scars. I watched Vratchken in her tight faded jeans, dark green jumper and a light grey hat with ear flaps, under which her jet black curls exploded in all directions. She moved like some creature, lean, muscular, rhythmical. She is a forest panther I thought.

Vratchken: Look at Killy staring over here. What does he see? A gangrel, glaikit speir-heidit quine an him sae dark against thi conifer wall. Fit a fair pile a trees, ah gie im at, an aa.

Killy shouted over. 'Hey, Vratch, some tea for energy?'

'Grand, aye, fine, ken.'

•   •   •   •   •   •   •   •   •   •   •   •   •   •   •   •   •

Vratchken and I sat down on a stump each, listening to the birds. A male blackbird hopped between us, his beak bright orange against the black ground. I could feel the sunny warmth of the dry stump coming up through my jeans. I handed Vratch a Thermos cup of sugared tea. She took her hat off and the anarchic hair sprang out like a jack-in-the-box. The sun glinted and haloed above her head: a dark angel.

'Killy this a first – Wolfclaw's first direct and illegal action. Are we daft or what?'

'Vratch, I'm enjoying this – cutting down trees

instead of planting them.'

'Ken fa owns them?'

'I think Lord and Lady Stubbington-Moles, scions of a vast tobacco fortune. They're nicknamed Lord and Lady Cancer. It's a grand tax dodge for them and they're never up here. They have a factor, a florid-faced git whose name I don't recall, but he's never here in the winter. In fact right now, he's skiing over in Aspen where he spends Christmas. He won't discover any of this until next spring, by which time the wolf pack will be howling elsewhere.'

'But what if we were caught?'

'A court fine, a week or two in jail, probably lose our jobs. Domestic disaster. Still, this soil could support a brilliant hardwood forest and all the wildlife that goes with it. These conifers grow so close together they choke off the light at the base and you won't find many insects, birds or flowers down there.'

The blackbird stared at us both and hopped to the stump between us. I imagined its perfect song-note frozen in the winter air, frozen only to thaw next spring, repeating itself over and over again, frozen in winter, thawed every spring.

We sawed, leaving the fallen trees in a regular trail. I thought of the absent Lord and Lady, sipping tea somewhere in Pimlico, a servant packing their bags for Bermuda, an accountant noting carefully the income from next year's Scottish timber plantation. I grinned at the accountant puzzling over a few missing trees. Still, I pity them who can't hear this blackbird sing here and now.

•   •   •   •   •   •   •   •   •   •   •   •   •   •   •   •   • · •   •

Cree Dan and Conger: Miles away, up another path, a more ruthless cutting. Red spruce, the paper pulp tree.

'Dan, how risky is this?'

'No risk at all. The owners live in South Africa and

the factor is in London, on his way to some rock festival in France. Greed works in our favour here. I love spruces and remember them from my childhood; bonnie trees in Colorado or Alberta. The Indians used to make beer from this one. These trees can do it all: turpentine, floorboards, tanning and pulp. Balance, man, balance. How many birds do we hear singing; no squirrels, pine martens or anything else. Even the deer must forage elsewhere. These Norway Spruce are ideal for Wolfclaw purposes though, Conger.'

'How's that?'

'They make ideal Christmas trees.'

• • • • • • • • • • • • • • • • • • •

I could leave the pub for a while in other hands, Killy had a full month off work, Vratch three weeks and Conger could pick his own hours. In three full days, part one was complete. The trees were all cut, waiting collection.

Big Tammas came in on the Thursday morning. 'Grand day' was all he said (all he ever said). Tammas, huge, greasy blue jeans of many colours, and brown rig boots encrusted with fish scales and mud.

I asked Tammas if his lorry was for hire, with him driving.

'Any cargo?'

'Umm, Tammas, just Christmas trees.'

'Where to?'

'Glasgow.'

• • • • • • • • • • • • • • • • • • •

We arrived at a waste lot in the east end of Glasgow on a cold December morning just after the worst of rush hour. It was a site Killy had directed us to as a 'trading' site, one he'd remembered from visits to his Donegal uncle who lived somewhere near. The lot was just off the main road; it was covered in litter, glass and rubble. Conger and I had come with Big Tammas, leaving Vratch and Killy to attend to other matters.

'Got the sign Conger?'

FOR SALE – XMAS TREES (PRICES ATTACHED TO EACH TREE)

We unloaded the trees, placing them around the lone crumbling brick wall, bounding the site (probably soon to be a parking lot). The Lodgepole Pines and Norway Spruce made a lovely collage of blue and green against the dark grey canvas of Glasgow fog.

• • • • • • • • • • • • • • • • • •

The trees disappeared the next day – so we'd heard – for all of us were well up the A9 by that time. We imagined them in the tenements and closes of Parkhead, Bridgeton and Gorbals Cross, folk puzzling over the attached 'price tags' which read: MERRY CHRISTMAS FROM YOUR NORTHERN FRIENDS: A FREE CHRISTMAS TREE TO BRIGHTEN YOUR DAY. PEACE ON EARTH!

And that was the cutting down phase. I could imagine the late Matt McGinn writing a song about the free Xmas trees in the east end of Glasgow and we chuckled at this gift from a Lord and Lady who weren't prone to giving gifts to anyone – welcomed tax breaks as their free right for which others paid.

While we were in Glasgow, Vratchken and Killy were preparing nice Xmas presents for the good citizens of Macqueensport.

(*And Ivan, a six-foot-six ploughman from the Chuvash brushed and clean, like an awkward schoolboy on prize-giving day, stood in the glitter and chrome of Heathrow Airport where a woman and girl both blonde as white birch trees came down a ramp into the light of the lounge where they first saw him. He was minded of their grey eyes and later, the big ploughman let his tongue and scrubbed clean fingers work over his woman's gentle flesh, like preparing the ground for seeding time; he knew that much and more – laughing and crying in their own tongue. 'Wait until you see the sky, wait until you see the sky' he said over and over again.*

London was waking just as these two were falling asleep, just as Big Tammas' lorry climbed the last hill into Macqueensport.)

The days leading to Christmas came hard and clean, icy days, bluest skies, calm seas, mountains glistening with frost. News of the Glasgow Christmas tree saga began to filter north, via aunties and brothers who were exiled in the city. Newspapers saw it only as an interesting filler, written up once, only to be forgotten:

O CHRISTMAS TREE
Glasgow police and residents are puzzled over a 'Christmas tree sale' in which trees were unloaded onto a waste site off London Road. The trees had tags which invited the reader to take the tree for nothing. Those delivering the trees disappeared. It appears to have been a harmless but generous prank, intended to supply free Christmas trees to needy families in Glasgow's East End. Police suppose the trees were surplus and were thus handily disposed of at no cost to the public.

•   •   •   •   •   •   •   •   •   •   •   •   •   •   •   •   •   •

Ivan and his wife and daughter arrived at the Haddock Arms a few days before Christmas and I showed them the flat. I could see their grey eyes brighten. I explained to Ivan that they were to rest and settle in until well after the New Year. I wanted Ivan to show them the village and countryside. Ivan could help me over the holidays by tending bar and learning the cellar and storage arrangements in the pub. He was a fast learner. The flat was private so gave this Chuvashi family all the freedom and comfort they would need. I sometimes heard crying at night but I had heard these tears all my life; the tears immigrants cry at night from Halifax to Vancouver Island – tears of longing.

•   •   •   •   •   •   •   •   •   •   •   •   •   •   •   •   •   •

If Santa rode out that year over believers and unbelievers, sceptics, drunkards, prophets and teetotallers – in his hallucinogenic magic mushroom shaman sleigh, his eagle eye would have had a feast over Macqueensport. Along the great burns below, separated into foam by great waterfalls, otters stripped brown trout of their firm flesh, and stoats, now in ermine, preyed on rats. Ptarmigan rose up over shivering blue hares, and blackbirds pecked the snow off rowan branches; bracken sleeping, heather glazed and still. Herds of red deer moved silently down the deep straths, feeding among ruined and crumbling shielings, their black formations like something from the African veldt, seeking branches from bare hazel and alder. All this under stars and moon so cold that a blow might shatter them like the ice choking the pools and lochans. He would hear children dreaming at the edge of this winter planet.

 • • • • • • • • • • • • • • • • • •

And the good citizens of Macqueensport awoke to a small birthday treat. On every porch or sheltered back garden was a wooden box of stripling trees for planting, each bundle tied with red ribbon. Many were oaks, some sprouting from acorns in small pots. On every piece of vacant ground grew a new tree; along the shore, at the base of every statue or war memorial: rowans, birches, hazel, elder, alder, blackthorn. Each bundle of trees told the story of each species, its history and folklore.

Make a flute, a spoon or a fork, a tool handle, a walking stick, a pot of wine. This tree wards off evil, it trembles with the second sight, it can break heads and bones, home to the cuckoo and the wild vision, the madman, the prophet and poet.

People said there had been oaks planted everywhere, with great care and precision, maybe at a time of year when trees shouldn't be planted; but most folk agreed more than just trees had been planted.

Chapter eleven

The weather changed after Christmas. The sky and hills turned a filthy grey. Horizontal rain belted against windows and doors. The sun was muted and never came out at all. Macqueensport lived under a dark blanket from morning to night. Folk even stayed away from the pub, preferring the warmth of their own fires. But it was a good time for the Wolfclaw who could gather in secret. It also gave everyone a chance to meet Ivan's family. Wife Anish, and daughter Sura, age eighteen, came into the Ruction Room, slate eyes happy and shy.

'These are my soul,' said Ivan proudly and quietly. We understood what he meant.

'We are verruh much pleased to ken you,' said Sura.

'We ken' laughed Vratchken, then everyone laughed.

'*Slainte – le durachdan*. Best wishes.'

Ivan hovered but I told him this was just a social visit, not Claw business. Ivan strode back to watch the bar. We got down to business.

'Full marks,' I began. 'Ivan is desperate to get some action but we have to let him ease into the life here first. We can't put him at risk when things begin to hot up.'

'How hot?' asked Killy.

'Let Conger say. Conger?'

'The *craicline* says things are still quiet. The Xmas presents were seen as a kind gesture from the Forestry people and some local landscape gardeners. No connections so far seen between Glasgow and the northern tree plantations. Local bobbies have enough to do with drink driving, bad roads and so on. It was great – us all in black, running around the village at 3 am. I knew the bobbies were forty miles up the road. The 'man with no name' told me. I protect my sources.'

'Ken, aye, but surely people are on tae us?'

I knew that and knew it too well.

'Vratch is right. This will lead to confrontation but the advantage of symbolic action is that most people see these acts only as a series of unrelated pranks. We made a point about trees. Now we move to our next 'project'. Killy, you're our man.'

Killy swirled his double whisky. He looked like a rock lizard, black and leathery, reading the future in his dark glass. His eyebrows were rising and falling like a seesaw, one going up while the other went down.

'Enough trees for now – enough oaks to keep the Druids happy for a few centuries. Enough birches and rowans to kickstart a new Caledonian forest. But I've got an idea for our next 'action'. Here's a story. A week before Christmas, my sister-in-law Morna was driving over the moors to do some shopping. Her nine-month-old daughter was strapped into a small child-seat in the back. It was cold. There was ice on the road. She was driving slowly, carefully. Then, two stags leaped from the hillside. One landed on the bonnet, the other on the windscreen. One deer actually came through the windscreen and ended up half in the passenger seat. It kicked its way out the car, leaving blood and entrails on the seat. The car spun off the road, into a huge boulder. The bairn was howling. The fuel line must have been severed because the car went up in flames just a few minutes after Morna got the baby out of the car. The car exploded. Morna got a lift home. Her husband reported this to the police but he also phoned the local laird. The laird told him the deer were wild creatures and thus not the responsibility of the estate.'

Conger practically choked on the words. 'They're his deer to be shot for thousands of pounds each by toffs from the south but not his when they eat our trees and vegetables. The deer fences to keep them off the roads are his responsibility and those fences are in helluva disrepair at the moment.'

'Well, the upshot is that the laird hung up on Morna's husband, while spluttering about having the best lawyers in Scotland. Not a word of apology or concern for Morna and her bairn. In a perfect ecology – minus sheep of course – wolves would eat sickly and elderly deer, culling the herds naturally. Let the Bambi Wars begin ...'

'We're no gonnae kill the beasts.' Vratch got up, returning to the table with a round of drinks. 'Nae need tae kill the beasts.'

'Conger?'

'It's a mercy to them. The herds suffer from overpopulation, which leads to starvation and disease. The estates have no incentive to repair fences or cull the deer for nothing. Hence, our cars, bairns and gardens suffer. The way I see it, natural justice demands that Morna deserves compensation for her suffering and her car, the same as if a lion or tiger escaped from a zoo and injured someone.'

Conger was animated in the weak light of the ruction room. Vratch was clearly agitated and angry, her eyes blazing, but lowered. Killy was still staring at the whisky glass.

'Forecast, Swami.'

'Right. I forecast lovely rich haunch of venison, roasting slowly in the oven, its rich gravy soaking into spuds, carrots and onions. I foretell Cree Dan slicing the lean venison into thin strips, soaking it in a rich marinade of herbs, smoking it over a slow oak fire to make the sweetest charqui, melting on the tongue. I see rich stews cooked in Dutch ovens on outdoor coals ... '

Vratchken wasn't pleased with Killy's carnivorous visions and she put forward an idea that we all agreed with finally. The one we used.

• • • • • • • • • • • • • • • • • • •

Ian Factor parked his Landrover at the bottom of the long, ice-coated track. He began his long walk up to the big house, where each morning, he stoked up the Rayburn to keep the house warm enough to avoid frozen pipes until the laird came up for Hogmanay and the week after. Factor was just turning the key in the door when he heard a commotion coming from the walled garden, the laird and his lady's pride and joy. Factor walked over the frozen grass to the right and rear of the house. His bloodshot eyes weren't really ready for what he saw there. A deer fence had been erected in a loop, blocking entry to the walled garden. The deer fence was necessary because at least a dozen red deer stags were munching the laird's herbs and rare alpines. The animals were content like munching cows, each stag snorting and rubbing its scent against the various shrubs and trees. Factor put his specs on to read the sign posted in the middle of the deer fence.

THIS IS A FINE EXAMPLE OF A HIGHLAND DEER FENCE IN GOOD REPAIR.
'GOOD FENCES MAKE GOOD NEIGHBOURS.'
The Bambi Liberation Front

Chronicles
Cree Dan:

These are mental chronicles, 'written' in my head only. We got big Tam's wagon again and drove into the Horseshoe Road and waited. Vratch, Killy, Conger and myself. We were well-hidden from view. Vratch had got these darts from somewhere, for tranquillising whale sharks for tagging purposes. Well, they worked. Conger is an excellent shot and we soon had at least a dozen Royals, silently shot and gathered from the moor. We had two helpers put up the fence meanwhile, just leaving an open corner for us to put the deer in. The deer came to slowly, then sluggishly began to explore the garden. They had plenty of room to feed, to get their bearings. We pitied them, but they looked at home against the backdrop of Scots pine and Douglas fir. I thought of Donnachadh Ban's poem:

My blessings on the foxes, because they eat the sheep.

I think. My blessings on the wolves, for they eat the deer, *which eat the people.*

We know that Ian Factor never told the laird. He couldn't but the message was clear to Factor at least. He persuaded the laird to have all the deer fences repaired.

So Lairdie, of the Name of Six Hyphens, your estate is judged by the number of stags it houses, to the tune of ten to fifteen thousand pounds per animal, each standing four feet high at the withers, sixteen stone, eight point, nine point, Royal, Imperial, each capable of eating twelve hundred pine seedlings a day, rutting, casting antlers. One hundred and fifty thousand beasts in 1963, double that by 1993. Cars, women and children being maimed on the roads but not you or your own, who don't go to our hospitals, schools and markets, who don't give anything, but take and take. Your taking days are over.

It was a helluva dream. We were herding the great stags and delicate hinds up from the snowy plateaux of Cairngorm, down into the great plains of Perthshire; out of the wild oaks of Ardnamurchan and Morvern; down from the straths of the far north, from the sweet grass of Meall na Moile, the sweeter waters of Cam and Veyatie. From the frozen edges of Tuath, I could see them from a great height. They moved in black spills down the deep gorges and corries, a slow hypnotic herding of great muscled beasts, tawny, dappled, chapped and wounded; they all moved like a great African migration of gazelle or wildebeest or North American elk or bison. They were being driven by all the people, herdsmen, stalkers, factory workers and thousands of homeless people out from the cities, emptying out from bus shelters and shopfronts, joining together, singing, talking, heading north, true north. I was above all this, maybe on a mountain though I recall no land beneath my feet. A man talked to me in Gaelic, dressed in an ancient green cloak and slanted hat:

> *S am buirean beag sgiolta*
> *Bu sgiobalt' air grine,*
> *Gun sgiorradh gun tubaist*
> *Gun tuisleadh gun diobradh*

He sang this song of the flight of the deer, of their fear and nimbleness, their slender grace, their sure-footedness ...

Then the people and deer came in vast arteries to a natural amphitheatre, where all the great deer came to the centre of the circle. The laughing and singing people grew silent. The stags began to paw the ground, nostrils flaring, the weak winter sun striking their antlers, seeming to set them on fire. Then the people melted away, the many thousands who had marched. The people had turned to wolves and the wolves began to howl. I awoke.

Others thought they were dreaming too.

Morna Mackenzie came back from the hospital to see a brand new Volvo parked in her driveway. It had a red ribbon tied around the aerial. In the passenger seat was a wrapped gift. She unwrapped it: a vacuum pack of smoked venison.

(How that happened is nobody's business; not for this or any chronicle.)

INTERLUDE:
Hogmanay revisited

Cree Dan: I will always be just half of anything but the half of me that is not Scottish does not care for any of it. A Presbyterian's wet dream, a Calvinist's blueprint. Take all of the bundles of guilt, inadequacy and fear multiplied by most of a nation's people and dole them out in one night of false bonhomie, false sentiment, whisky-inspired randiness and bullshit, entertaining people you can't stand or who wouldn't let you in their front door normally; groping smelly uncles and prim Aunt Grundies (you may have to kiss them); throw in some football bigotry and sectarianism, drink driving and lies and more lies, resulting in:

> Fights
> Domestic strife
> Syrup sentimentality for things that never were
> The DTs

Imagine a cheerless Protestant nation with no clear sense of joy trying a night of good cheer, humour, song and dance; a nation that despises all feeling as frippery and hates the bedrock of any real emotions including love and hate. A recipe for disaster on the grand scale!

The *rest* of the year should be Hogmanay: a release from truth, joy, music, dance and song. Flush away the whisky and rum, the thin lager, all drinks dark and light FLUSH THEM DOWN and leave these dark dangerous children to look each other in the eye, just for once, and tell the truth. The 'rebels' are all drunk or stoned, slurping beer, farting and belching. The Roman Emperor who wished mankind had just one neck to sever; no need, Caesar, simply give the children piss to drink. Opium of the Masses. Firewater. Did my people in, more powerful than the carbine, the smallpox, left them bloated and impotent, thinking they were enjoying themselves, indeed, even rebelling against something! My people lying in the gutters of every western city and town. Firewater. And for nearly twenty years I have been peddling the stuff, poisoning my townspeople. I the flabby warrior-hypocrite, lard ass arselicker in a nation of arselickers.

So in the Haddock Arms, they will spend, drink, fart and belch, talk crap, hate themselves, covet. Manitou help us, help me. They will sing songs about bravery and nationhood, and I will sweep up the puke, the broken glass and fag ash; not one new thing will be said, worse, not one honest thing will be said so maybe I will say it now. I am a liar but an honest liar. Caledonian Antisyzygy.

No more firewater. The purest water on earth is under our feet. Let's drink it.

Stop jerking off – tell the truth.

Tell someone else the truth.

Play your own jig, dance your own dance.

Get high? Look at Orion.

I do not say YOU I say WE. I do mean (WE.)

On the 30th of December, I turned the pub over to Killy and Ivan and spent four days alone in a disused coastal war bunker, doing war with my own thoughts. These were the darkest four days of my life but I won in the end, celebrating by holding a glass of pure water up to Orion and drinking it in a oner.

Chapter twelve

The winter truly began. Deep snow fell on the hills, drifting across the roads, but the days stayed clear and crisp. Each of the Wolfclaw had their own work to attend to. Killy was on a long holiday from his own planting and stayed up in his cottage, reading, telling stories to his kids and catching up on needed DIY.

Vratch was working hard on the pier, supervising the ebb and flow of the fish-selling industry.

High winds kept Conger island-bound for the most part.

Most important to me, Ivan, Anish and Sura were settling in very well, always eager to please and learning more English every day. Ivan had become indispensable and was able to do any practical task. He was a steady barman too, and very popular with the locals. He freed me from many pub tasks I didn't like doing. We closed the pub a few weeks in January and gave the place a thorough cleaning and redecorating, something it hadn't had in twenty years. While cleaning the chimney one day, I saw big Ivan's brow furrow.

'I am thanking you with everything I have. I have freedom again and will one day be on the Scottish land where I belong.'

'How is your family?'

'They both feel the same and sometimes feel they are not giving enough in return.'

'Nonsense, Ivan, man, they never stop cleaning and cooking. I would like them to take over the kitchen completely and serve up good Chuvashi fare. This pub has been an eyesore for too long and we have never done pub meals.'

Ivan paused at his work.

'Remember what I vowed. I would never betray the Wolfclaw but I want to get involved. If there is a risk I must take the risk and Anish and Sura understand that too. If you knew us and our life in that State, we have always done what you are doing now, taking risks, winning symbolic victories against our oppressors. If you protect us too much, Dan, we lose self-respect. You fear too much in the West. Ourselves, from the day we are born, know we will grow old and die. Natural. No man can really harm us. We also have what seems to you a strange notion of friendship. It is a point of honour to die for your friends and we have done that silently and firmly for centuries. You are not asking me to die for you, merely to help you with your dreams.'

He looked up then.

'No Cree Dan, do not protect me anywhere. Besides I am a landsman, a true changing wolf. And I am one of you. '

I knew he was right and clasped his big hand.

Ivan's family shamed me with their pride in the place. Everything was repaired and clean, furniture mended, fixtures and fittings replaced, dusted, polished, glistening. It was then I noticed Ivan's attraction to tools of any kind. In the pub, he nearly went into a trance with a pair of pliers or some kitchen utensil. In a few days, I saw how handy this passion for tools could be.

• • • • • • • • • • • • • • • • • • •

Ivan and Conger were far less subtle in their approach than Killybegs and myself: they were advocates of direct Highland action. Ivan had a fetish about tools for cutting, snipping, ripping. (Too long with the mackerel, we reckoned.) He had an old Lada Riva toolbag (supplied with the car) stamped with Cyrillic letters which Ivan said meant 'cut the bastard open'. His kit contained bolt cutters and a lethal hacksaw. Conger behind the wheel of a blue N-reg. Ford Escort scouring the country roads for NO TRESPASS, KEEP OUT, PRIVATE ESTATE signs. Cut bolts, hack chains. Ivan had an impressive bag of padlocks and chains which he slowly restored and took away for storage for whatever purpose. This night was a soft rain. The pale moon swam in its sheen.

The gate would not budge.

'Easy man, easy,' said Conger, his nose dripping down his ripped oilskins. Ivan swears through his beard, in a disturbing rising crescendo:

'zha, ZHA, ZHIZHIN, SHSCHIT, SHSCHIT ...'

He rattles the chains which sets dogs barking and lights shining from the nearby house; the chain works loose and the boys resort to the old Highland trick of lifting a locked gate off its hinges; then Ivan stands in the rain like Atlas, spinning the wrecked gate over his head and heaving it far out into the burn, knocking a PRIVATE FISHING ONLY sign into the burn with it. The gate points heavenward for an instant, then sinks; the two run squelching over the slippery dying bracken. Ivan curses the padlock that got away ...

• • • • • • • • • • • • • • • • • • •

After that, Big Ivan was irrepressible. His own English got raunchier and more experimental, egged on by various regulars in the bar.

'Shit fire ... and save matches.'

'Bad blue jeans? Aye, because CHERKNOB'LL FALL OOT!'

'A haddie, horosho, a right fuckin haddie.'

'Aye, a grand cunt of a night, grand cunt of a night.'

I could see, though, that Ivan would never be excluded again, whatever the risk. Maybe, ultimately, his strength would be a decider, his fearlessness would take us over any rough patches.

As the winter wore on, we had plenty of kindlers for the pub fires. Ivan brought in a steady stream of

PRIVATE, KEEP OUT and NO ANGLING signs which we stored in the coal shed until needed.

Anish and Sura were great. They simply did what needed done. They were very happy in their own flat. They also took over the kitchen with my blessing and did away with the expected scampi, filled rolls, greasy chips. Delicious soups crept in, and new ways of doing lamb and fish. All this warmth was something out of an old Russian novel. Food, spice, drink and laughter in front of a roaring fire while outside, the earth turned to iron and the sea battered the shoreline, keeping everybody off work for weeks.

Chronicles:

I love this cold because I was born to it. Born *in* it. Cold, because it cherishes warmth: ice over water, living roots under the tundra, fish deep under the frozen lochan and turbulent waves. This is only a respite during a dark and frozen winter. Our team is merely taking a breather, a recess. There is a change too in the seugh and sigh of the wind.

There is a thaw coming and spring is turning in its sleep.

Chapter thirteen

Conger, Killy and I set off in Conger's old blue Ford one day in early February. The road was clear and dry but the hills were covered in a hard frost, waterfalls frozen and heather covered in a glaze of ice. We drove north. Conger was effusive.

'The most beautiful land on earth, especially on a clear February day.'

'Even Donegal never looked like this and I've never seen it in ice,' added Killy.

I had to agree with Conger who gave a running commentary as we continued north. My memory was stretched, trying to remember the houses and people we passed but Conger knew it all.

'Ledi died in 73, left this to his brother in New Zealand and it was sold from there as a holiday home two years later. It's sometimes rented from October to March, lived in a few months in the summer. The Rowans? Has been a pottery, a stable, a craft shop, fishing lodge, knocked down for a bungalow ...'

I'd known Conger for twenty years. His father and mine had gone to school together and were distant cousins in fact, but I never knew this part of Conger's brain or his muted bitterness. I felt more Cree then and could see his ancestral lands as I could see mine. Conger was going way back now.

'School, now ruin ... '

'Old smithy now a riding school ... '

And we saw the fenced houses, glistening white in the February sun, surrounded by ornamental shrubs and Lawson cypress. We stopped in a lay-by, where Conger lifted a cardboard box of sandwiches and a Thermos flask from the boot. We got out of the car. Killy poured hot tea from the flask, the steam lingering in the cold air. We looked over the frozen moor to the ice-ringed hills. I could hear geese grazing from the distant river. Crows cackled in the stillness. An old lochside cemetery was framed between a Scots pine and the hills beyond.

'*Our people are there, Dan* – Macleods, Mackenzies, Macraes – a hard life in a wondrous place. I remember once rowing around that loch with the man now buried under that Celtic Cross. We called him Bronco because he'd worked out west as a young man. Bronco taught me a lot that day. He worked for the local estate and we were netting fish with eel nets. God, man, the size of the brown trout we were bringing in. Some fifteen pounds or more. Bronco put a dozen or more of the biggest trout in a coal bag and said 'for your mum, now. That's for the work that was in it.' Those old men from here – on a loch like this, from hills like these – had to go away. Your father did, Dan. Imagine having to go away from here. Bronco told me his uncle was ghillie to the man who caught the biggest brown trout in Scottish history, right off the end of that island.'

All of us looked to the west of the loch.

Killy waved his hand toward the island. 'That island is covered in native trees like hazel, alder and native pine. Lots of native flowers and herbs, wild garlic and insect-eating flowers, all because sheep and deer couldn't get out there to graze. Some botanists say these islands show us what the mainland looked like before sheep grazing and deer parks.'

We sipped more hot tea.

Conger's hot tea breath blew out like a smoking dragon.

'I have an idea about these holiday houses. A grand idea I got from thinking about Bronco.'

'Burn them,' added Killy, 'like the Welsh – but that would be a helluva mockery to the people that built them.'

'No Killy, something, better and more lasting,

perfectly legal and nothing gets burned.'

Conger didn't say much on the way back but I knew his mind was gathering, collating, filing away. This was the real Highland mind at work; a computer run by bitterness and memory.

• • • • • • • • • • • • • • • • • • •

Conger's List

No, I didn't say much on the way back. My thinking had gone underground, was tapping into something more, an idea, a *list*.

Thorntree. Built 1884; empty in 1954. Macrae, Tasmania I think.

Seaview. Cleared 1820s. Two roofless ruins. Land belongs to some upper-class twit.

Three shielings and two roofless outbuildings. Cleared 1830s. Canada. Now part of Hyphen-Hyphen's estate.

A grassy sward, bounding the river, gone to upper New York State. Fishing rights now estate's.

From the hill, see where the reeds advance on the lime green fields. Cleared to Nova Scotia. Macrae and five children.

This list is slow and depressing. So familiar and final. God's will, the people's will, destiny, fate. But this is leading somewhere. I am a logical crofter, son of a logical crofter. Forced eviction and violence was legal then, would be illegal now. Since we can't legislate for then, we can legislate for now. **Legal reparation, compensation**.

I made lots of lists. I had a list of all the houses in the seven major straths spoke-wheeling out from Macqueensport: out of 309 houses, 121 were holiday homes, legally held by absentees who had legally acquired them from local folk: my own kith and kin. Those homes could be well-used by people like myself, or even teachers, mechanics, rural workers whose sons and daughters would help reactivate the school. A mind game. I take a list of eager tenants. Make them house keys. Leave them keys to occupy the places until the BMWs and new Landrovers drive up in the spring or a few weeks at Hogmanay. Let the shit hit the fan. The logic of Macqueensport versus that of Kensington or Morningside, head-on. History, economics, accountancy put through the meat grinder of passion and necessity, pleasure and leisure. What a fuckin mess that would be but who would ever clear it up?

Instead, I took my list to Fiery John who lived in a bungalow near the kirkyard. Fiery John was nearly eighty. He had been a merchant seaman, infantryman, jute mill foreman in India. There was nothing unusual about the bungalow, inside or out.

Conger, man, come in and Happy New Year to you – *bliadhna mhath ur, a bhailaich.*

Tapadh leibh, and yourself John.

A wee sensation?

Yes thanks.

I need help, John.

How so, Conger?

For reasons of my own, I need to know more about the people on this list.

I gave him the list.

'Aye, so.' He peered over his spectacles and oohed and aahed, shifting occasionally, fingering his bottle, shuffling his feet.

'So, I can do it, Conger. I have most of it up here in my grey head and the rest on my shelves. But what is it, Conger? What's the meaning of it?'

'I'll tell you as soon as I can.'

A few weeks later I saw John on the shore and he gave me a big envelope. I took it to the library and opened it. It was all there. He had photocopied some maps and by means of coloured pens, had each part of the map coded to a list of names arranged in alphabetical order under the following countries:

> Australia
>
> Canada
>
> New Zealand
>
> South Africa
>
> United States

and others which included Brazil, Indonesia and Mozambique.

I gave Fiery John two bottles of his favourite (he refused everything else). In exchange, I got something of immense value to the Wolfclaw.

I'm no typist but I did prepare a rough copy of a letter on my old typewriter to give to someone with a computer.

Dear,

Our records establish that you are the direct legal heir to land which was taken from your forebears without just compensation. This land has been held for two hundred years as result of violence and eviction. The direct line is listed below:

> *1.*
>
> *2.*
>
> *3.*
>
> *4.*

If you are interested in taking up this matter, please inform us. We also have a list of local people who could use this land if you wish to sign it over to them. Feudal and smallholding systems unique to Scotland mean this land has no great value, nor would you be able to use it in any practical way. Any romantic or sentimental attachments you may have to the land might better be translated by seeking further legal advice on the matter. Enquiries to L.W.S. Mackenzie, Solicitor, Destitution Road, Glasgow G1.

Mackenzie, my first cousin, said it could be a landmark attempt and was confident of its legal success. He said it would revolutionize landholding in the Highlands. Legal pals with a knowledge of crofting law said it could return valuable land to the townships.

Mackenzie said within the month, he had received over two hundred replies from every province in Canada, thirty-seven American states, and stamps from countries his stamp-collecting children had never seen before. Simply, most of the replies said: 'go right ahead, kinsman'.

Chronicles:

So Cree Dan, back at the Haddock Arms. Insomnia, I can hear wee mice in the walls. I am thinking of many things. I think of the old stonemason Donald MacLeod from Strathnaver who witnessed the clearances from his native strath. MacLeod taught himself to write so that he could tell the whole world what he truly saw:

'... no language that I am able to use can convey an adequate idea of the wrongs and sufferings of my unfortunate countrymen, but silence in the face of such a mess of cruelty and iniquity would be enough *to make the very stones cry out ...*'

The very stones cry out.

He saw them cleared from Rossal, Badinloskin, from Loch nan Clar. In 1819, smoke from the cottages being burned blinded sailors miles out at sea.

The Cree would know it, and the Assiniboine and a thousand peoples whose tongues were cut out.

I think of my old man, working out west; a sociable man, but sometimes as lonely as a planet and I think of where he came from and his grave being covered by dry dust and prairie snow; buried among total strangers. If he came back here to die, he would have been buried among total strangers too.

Conger knew those things too. That's why he was silent on the drive back.

'Gloomy Memories' MacLeod told the story of his

clearances until the establishment began to actually listen to the stonemason – began to hear the cadences of a prophet not those of a madman. Then Donald MacLeod just disappeared, vanished, 'circa 1857'. MacLeod is probably covered under a skyscraper or parking lot in Toronto.

It is enough to make the very stones cry out.

I think the other day, Conger heard the stones crying.

Chapter fourteen

A quiet February night in the Haddock Arms. All Wolfclaw, including Ivan.

I'm afraid to say I did not look on Vratchken as a Wolfclaw sister; she had on a floral peasant dress, a kind of pinafore. She had on suede boots. She was stunning, dark, smouldering. Lord have mercy! Manitou protect me! The fire flickered. Hail pounded the windows. I opened the meeting.

'I think we've had a good winter's work but a good rest too. Now is the time to draw up a spring offensive. Myself, I've had enough of trees for the moment.'

'Cree Dan, it's not trees burning in that fire,' said Killy, pointing at the fireplace.

We all turned to look just as a PRIVATE – NO FISHING sign crackled and sputtered in the fire. The black paint melted, then whooshed up in a bright red flame.

'Symbolic act if ever I saw one,' said Conger.

I continued.

'Conger's got a long-term legal project on holiday homes but it's a legal process now and needs a lot more research, right Conger?'

'Aye. It will take time but it is more than symbolic. Property taken *illegally* can only be restored *legally*. The legal heirs of that land arc scattered all over the world. But the paperwork is rolling in. It should be a year or two before anything happens. The beauty of the whole thing is that it will be perfectly legal – beating the buggers at their own game.'

Vratch threw back her head, a handful of shiny curls coming away from her eyes.

'Spring brings trout and angling and I'd like to see us do something on the ancient angling rights of the Scottish people. The right to fish estuaries and rivers for native fish.

We could have a 'fish-in' for flounders. Scots folk have always had the right to fish tidal burns and rivers as far upstream as ordinary spring tides. That means we can fish the Liobag for trout. Know any fat rainbow trout pools? Under recent law, rainbows aren't classed as freshwater fish, so we can fish for them as well. So boys, tight lines.'

'Conger, can you give us the state of the opposition?'

'Well, Lord Hyphen-Hyphen has got the local bobbies steamed up. He thinks there is going to be a peasant uprising. Factor has no idea. Thinks it's some Gollachs or Glasgow anarchists. The Xmas trees may never even be noticed. Remember, it will be a Hielanman who discovers them – a gardener or forester – and he'll cover his own arse by not reporting it. I wouldn't worry too much on that score.'

Killy stared into his dark stout.

'I think we'll cross that line soon. We came close with the deer episode. My sister-in-law loves her new car, no questions asked. No offence, but this Irishman thinks we may need to open our ranks to new members with new ideas or else we'll knacker ourselves. Families, jobs and more work, come spring. Sorry Claw, but that's the way I feel.'

'Aye, gweed, ah cuid hae some quine company, ken.'

Conger interrupted.

'This is tricky. I think we have what we need. No more wolves for me. We're tight. I know this place. People will find out about us, but they'll find out a lot sooner if we take anyone else on board. Also, we have to think about Ivan. Our team is big enough – for his sake alone. More people would put him at risk. Gossip. Rumour.'

Ivan grew agitated at this. 'Don't worry about me. I am a *tovarisch* – a comrade. I could not stay here under any other terms.'

I called for a vote to our 'recruitment' drive. Killy. *For*. Ivan *For*. Vratch. *For*. Conger. '*Dead set against.*' I hedged, '*for, with reservations.*'

'Any names already in the hat?'

'Big Tam the Driver has helped us already.'

'He's just for hire. He'd hire his rig for any purpose.'

Killy put his wife forward.

Conger: 'Too much risk, Killy. When we get caught, somebody has to stay out of jail. You and Ivan have family. The rest of us can afford a few risks. Besides, telling any recruits what we're up to already gives out more information and suppose they don't join? Catch 22.'

I told Conger we had to try.

'Not so easy up here, Dan. Vested interests, kinship, gossip, the Almighty Craic. Let's wait and see how it goes in time. Let's get our own act together first.'

I felt uneasy about all of it ... thinking that it was more work we needed, not more people. More ideas. Killy and Ivan had families. Conger was the most local and his opinion counted for more. I leaned his way, thinking of our organic and spontaneous beginnings. I didn't think we could keep this going artificially. Also, so far, we'd escaped any real notice or trouble. We trusted one another completely.

But maybe we were too cozy, too smug. Vratch and Killy's jobs would really get hectic in a few months. I agreed with Conger and maybe secretly shared his guilt that we felt uneasy with our kinsmen and women; that we couldn't open to them.

• • • • • • • • • • • • • • • • • •

I got up early the next day. Ivan and his family had to go away to London for a few weeks. I woke to a pub freshly decorated, trig and glistening.

There was a loud knock at the back door. I opened it to a man with a briefcase.

He was tall, balding, thin grey hair, piercing blue eyes.

'CID. May I speak to Daniel Macrae please?'

'I'm Dan Macrae. People here call me Cree Dan.'

I let him in.

'Tea or coffee?'

'Tea please. No sugar or milk.'

We sat down in the wall seats around the corner of the bar.

'Thank you for the tea. Do you know much about Christmas trees, Mr Macrae?'

'Yes. I *like* Christmas trees. Lodgepole pines are lovely but I'm allergic to them.'

'How much would one pay for a lodgepole pine these days?'

'Five pounds or so. Some are sold with enough root to transplant afterwards.'

'Ideal. Should they be given away?'

(I think. Shit. Here we go. CID 6. Cree Dan 0. His eyes. I wish he would turn them off.)

'Not if they can be sold for a fiver.'

'How do you feel about giving them away to poor people in Glasgow's East End?'

'An act of charity, in keeping with the true Christmas spirit.'

He wrote in a notebook.

'Do you know anything about red deer, Mr Macrae?'

'Yes, I know they are lovely creatures. Strong, brave, graceful, muscular. Everything I'm not.'

'Do you hunt them?'

'I don't own a rifle. I hunted elk in Canada years ago.'

'Are you Canadian, Mr Macrae?'

'I'm a dual national.'

'Hmmm, I see.'

'My late father was a Scot, from here.'

He placed the empty teacup to the side and

opened his briefcase. The lock opened with a loud click. He cleared his throat. I knew what was coming next.

'Do you know much about wolves?'

'I … I … like them as animals. Quite common in Canada. They're extinct here. Communal, intelligent, cunning. It's a shame they're extinct in Scotland.'

'A shame?'

(His eyes brightened. I swear I could feel their heat.)

'Aye, a bloody shame.'

'I see, Mr Macrae.'

He snapped his briefcase shut. He rose quickly, pushing his chair back in. He offered his hand. I shook it. My palm was sweating.

'Thank you for the tea. I'll let myself out. Good morning.'

I heard the engine start; the car tyres on the gravel. I went to the bar and poured a double Glenmorangie, downed it in a oner.

I poured another one and watched the snow fall outside, each flake melting into puddles of rain.

I knew all the local bobbies. Easy-going normal men who played shinty and took their kids swimming and fishing and could talk easy over an off-duty pint. They could do the business too, when they had to, but generally had no grandiose notions of their work. There was a big turnover – normal in the Highlands – every five years or so, up to a certain rank. I never felt we would get trouble locally. The big estate owners whinged elsewhere and had connections higher up – elsewhere. I saw only two options now: retreat quietly, cut our losses. Or charge into the teeth of it. For me, there could only be one answer. No fresh recruits. My memory told me what to do.

Chronicles:

Many years ago, I saw a television programme about the last

continuous band of prairie bison. This buffalo herd lived up near the Territories, in Northern Alberta. Wolves had also lived up there continuously, from prehistoric times. The wolves studied the buffalo patiently, noting the weak old bulls, the sickly cows, the new calves. A buffalo kill could feed the pack for several days and could also mean the difference between life and starvation. A buffalo could gore a wolf to death, kick its brains out, stomp it bleeding into the frozen ground. The buffalo were always aware of the wolves, always on guard. Their vigilance balanced perfectly with the wolf vigilance and had done so for thousands of years. The buffalo flourished and the wolves flourished. The top male wolf takes the lead in the hunt. He must keep up pressure or else lose respect but he must never make a rash mistake and lose his life. His death would affect the delicate balance of the pack at a time when survival was the only issue. A lone wolf could not kill an adult buffalo. Wolves had to attack the softer flesh to the rear of the animal as a pack – and hang on.

That day, on television, I remember the pack was starving, lean, nervous. The wolves finally cornered a buffalo cow near a fast-flowing creek. They didn't let her leave the water. Each time she tries to leave, the wolf leader snaps at her face, risking her horns. He won't let her get up the muddy bank. She is tiring, slipping in the mud. Finally, she decides to swim away. The wolves swim in after her. They sink their teeth into the soft rear haunches and tear huge strips of flesh from her. They pass the flesh to the wolves waiting on the shore. These wolves take the meat back to the pack. The cow is panicking and thrashing in the creek, which is now foaming with blood. The wolves hang on. Once enough flesh has been taken, the wolves eat the cow, alive. She is slowly drowning. They finally drag her, breathing her last, to the creek bank.

I was repulsed at the whole thing and hated what the wolves were doing. They were methodical. The cow was in great pain, despite natural release of a type of blood anaesthetic which eased the pain in her final minutes.

A carcass is left under the northern sun. Geese fly overhead, the cold river flows on. Life gets back to normal. The buffalo graze and the wolves begin to prowl again.

In the Wolfclaw, I have never thought of myself as a leader in a rank or pecking order. I'm in awe of the rest of our group. Intelligence, strength and power. None of it mine. I feel like a misfit or a coward, belonging nowhere, least of all here. But I also know I have to act. My visitor changed the whole script. I must bite into the thrashing buffalo and though it drown me, I will not let go, for the sake of the pack.

INTERLUDE

There is a road in Northern Manitoba. It winds through the grey tundra. It goes past a clearing, surrounded by thin, wind-riven birch trees. There used to be an old caravan there. The caravan had one end cut off. A buffalo hide tipi was fastened to that end of the caravan. Smoke came out of the hole in top of the tipi. My mother often walked that road with me. She held my hand. We went through the caravan door. The caravan smelled like mushrooms. It was empty and dark. She sat me at the table, giving me a glass of juice and a bag of peppermints. She had brought these things. She walked through a caravan door which lead to the tipi. She stayed there as long as it took me to eat slowly through the bag of mints. She came out. Her eyes sparkled, her face was shining. There was never any sound. The wind sometimes shook the caravan. Sun came through its small windows. Dust danced in the rays. I tried to count the specks of dust, imagining them to be men flying through the light, only to disappear onto the dark floor of the caravan.

As a boy, I had often seen the power of strong drink, of herbs and drugs. Of drumming and singing. The tipi was none of those things. It was the power of starvation. I'd seen it in the older people. I think the tipi was nothing more than the joy at the end of several days of sweating and hunger; maybe the joy at a handful of berries or wild nuts.

So dead mother, what should I do now?

Ivan would be away for two weeks. That would be enough. **PUB CLOSED DUE TO ILLNESS.**

My room. Room enough.

Name: Daniel Macrae
Nationality: British and Canadian
Birthplace: Manitoba, Canada
Age: 40

Height: 5' 10''
Weight: 13 stone
Build: stocky
Distinguishing marks: Scar, right shoulder. Scar, left calf.
Eyes: blue
Hair: black
Complexion: reddish brown (ie new copper penny)
Languages spoken: Cree, Assiniboine, English, Gaelic, French
Occupation: publican

I took to my bed, with a jug of water and a clean glass at my bedside.

DAY ONE: Head full of food, belly empty. Some belly pain and weakness.
DAY TWO: Feel fresh, clean. Urine dark. Mouth smells, legs weak.
DAY THREE: Urine still dark, headache, gums sore, mouth smells, limbs weak.
DAY FOUR: General weakness, light-headed, constant thinking of food.
DAY FIVE: Knees weak, feel giddy, urine clearing. No headache. Gums tingling. Breath foul.
DAY SIX: Urine normal, sore gums, legs weak, light head, very tired. Sleep easy.
DAY SEVEN: Tired, weak, slept and dreamt.

I stand in front of my mirror, naked. My hair is matted, drenched in sweat. My mouth and tongue are different, even my lips have lost weight. My ribs are showing. I feel stronger; more powerful and confident. My mind is very clear. I know what to do now.

I feel my mother's hand. We walk down the long road, red in the sinking sun.

That road in Northern Manitoba. The road that

never ends.

> I take a long hot bath and drink a cup of tea.
> I go downstairs to the world.

Chapter fifteen

Killy: I told my wife Rowena a bit about Wolfclaw. She was polite, bemused. In favour of the idea, generally. 'God knows we need something. But one martyr in the family is enough. I'll visit you in jail as often as I can.'

Visit me in jail. I hinted at recruits and she thought we had things about right.

'Vratch has the most beautiful legs in Scotland.'

Not wolves, *felines* I thought. We both agreed I hadn't been around long enough to judge local recruits. I knew plenty Donegalmen (and women) would rise to the challenge. I put it on the back burner.

• • • • • • • • • • • • • • • • • • •

Vratch: A fuckin laugh, recruits ah mean. Are we no daft eneuch, ken? I thocht oan mah office mates. Middle-aged, pot-bellied, fitba an booze. Real Scotsmen, oglin tits an bums, belchin, fartin. Recruits, *tae a life*, mebbe. Ahm a truthful quine, ken? Women are different. Macqueensport quines are wives an mithers, hard-heidit, practical lassies. Naw. It's me an thi lads, gweed lads they are.

• • • • • • • • • • • • • • • • • • •

Conger: Recruits to what? Fearties, priest-ridden, minister-harried, opiate of the masses? Try drink, football, fighting, working. Let me say it as a local man. Going, going gone to Glasgow, London, Toronto, Sydney, Auckland. Tongues up the laird's arses, up the RSPB, the factor's arse, the Red Deer Commission's. None of my own generation, wherever they are. A few old men. Fishermen? Cockneys, Yorkshiremen, east Coasters. Brave fishermen. We'll have to fight our own corner. My world is the Island and I will fight for it. Sorry man, I've got a lover's quarrel with this whole thing.

• • • • • • • • • • • • • • • • • • •

Ivan: I will bring them on. These, our tribesmen. The Chuvashi poets, warriors, landsmen, ploughmen. I don't have anyone else here and I see the same thing in this land. I see fear but I see courage too. I have told my own two beloveds. They are birds of passage. I do not wish to trouble them much.

• • • • • • • • • • • • • • • • • • •

Cree Dan. Vision Recipe.

Down that Manitoba road many plants grow. Take the three-leaved plant of purple bloom. In spring, it is the roots you need. Take only the thin bark of the tree next to it and the blossoms of the red flowers on the left side of the road. These in a measure I can't quite recall. Beat them into a pulp. Dry the pulp. Drink it as tea. I drank three cups before the recruitment 'feedback' meeting. We were all there, the Wolfclaw, but many besides. I saw them through eyes being whipped by exploding dreams. I had the clear vision of a *madman*.

• • • • • • • • • • • • • • • • • • •

Big Ivan was talking in his own language to a man of remarkable appearance. The man was taller than Ivan, who was himself nearly six feet six. This man was so thin his black jeans barely hung on his bony hips. His hair was lank and black like an Indian's. He had dark skin. He wore a green blouse-shirt. His hands sliced the air like karate chops. His dark eyes glistened, streaming with tears. The discussion seemed friendly.

'Come here Dan, I want you to meet a friend of mine. A hero of mine.'

The dark man turned quickly like a snake. He looked down at me, extending his hand. He spoke in a thick, fluid English.

'I am Murgan. That means "snowstorm" in my own language.'

Ivan spoke. 'He is a poet and madman – a good madman.'

Murgan leaned back, chanting softly. It was like a hypnotic mantra.

atai, ataijos, bes derli,
bes derli, inmar-ebyr,
gep murgan, gep murgan.
Gord val, gord val, iman, iman,
jablok, oh jablok, jam jag.
Jam jag, jam jag, gurtyn gurt.
Murt, ug-murt, bad tseri …

There was silence, then applause. The dark slick of Murgan faded into the crowd.

'That was amazing, Ivan, what was it?'

'Many languages, rare languages. I did not know all of them. Some words only. It was a praise to his homeland; its trees, fruits and grains. A spell against all who would harm them. He glows at the idea of Wolfclaw. He wants to help.'

Standing to Ivan's left was a man I did recognize. A short, stocky man, oddly dressed. He came forward with Ivan.

He held out his hand.

'Mikhail Aleksandrovich …'

'Bakunin?'

'The same, brother.'

'But you died in 1876.'

'Only symbolically.' He was grinning.

'How … why … here?'

'I've run so fast that I'm in a state of preservation, perpetual motion. Ivan says I'm needed in the Scottish Highlands, pre-millennium. So here I am. Have Anarchist – Will Travel.'

'Why?'

'Why? Always why? We were not put on earth to ask questions. We were put on earth to act. I was old enough on the barricades to see that only direct action is the solution. Everything else is reform, dribble from the master's mouth. After 1848, I was sentenced to death, pardoned, returned to Russian to spend ten years in prison, was exiled to Siberia. I escaped to Japan, travelled through America, then to Europe. Man, you would not believe my adventures among pimps, civil war deserters, lunatics. Depravity of every kind.'

'Your hated State won then. It put you on the run.'

'No brother, the State doesn't exist. Look at your Highlands. The State follows but the rebel is always a step ahead. The state must *react* to the rebel, not vice versa. The action comes first, the reaction second so the rebel is always superior to the State. You are a cause, the State merely an effect.'

'Drink, Mikhail?'

'Tea please. I developed a taste for it in prison. Tea, for I am truly Russian.'

The crowd was surging like an amoeba under a microscope. It was a fancy dress ball covered in smoke, breathing in all accents and languages. The lights were dim. I brought Bakunin's tea to him. He was standing in the corner alone, once Europe's most wanted man. He took the tea, sipping slow like a parched animal in a desert oasis.

'Thanks, brother. Listen, I spent years in a fine home. I was a well-respected Officer in the Imperial Army. Prison life was no different than army life. In prison, I met a man who thought he was a wolf. I drank tea with spirit-wrestlers, fire worshippers, true believers, fasting holy men. But these mad men were harmless. They shared bread and water with me, nursed my illnesses. They felt sorry for my fine hands and weaker limbs. But the Army ... the Army ... was both mad and dangerous because it had power. It was an agent of power.'

I asked him: 'But when does it stop? This perpetual rebellion against the State? It always stops with prison, exile, death. The State always wins. It beats you in the end, ironically, in your case, using Karl Marx as its henchman.'

Bakunin smiled. He was beaming. He put his teacup back on the table.

'The State never wins. It never catches up. It hasn't caught me yet. Marx was an arse-licker who secretly wanted everything he said he hated. I knew this. That is why he expelled me from the International. I wouldn't be surprised if he was the one who first said about me: "On the first day of the revolution, Bakunin would be a treasure. On the second day, he should be shot." Marx never liked life with the people. I did, and still do.'

'You once said the passion for destruction is also a *creative* passion.'

'The Highlands prove it. This situation was created by greed. The vast sporting estates, the cleared townships. It will be destroyed by greed, by the arrogance of greed which will provoke the people. Why do you seek permission for everything from the very people who don't even want you there? Quit fuckin around brother. Eat *their* salmon. Cut down *their* fences. Pull down *their* signs, shoot *their* deer. Let them put you in prison. You might learn something. Listen, Wolfclaw is it? Perfectly happy, federative, cooperative, non-political associations. I kept telling Marx that. He could never understand the *non-political* idea. The Highlands is perfect for these things. You have great potential. I've been talking to Ivan about this. But you are so far driven by fear, not by passion. Every destructive act will, in time, become a creative one. It is the alchemy of action. It will happen. A tight, small, organised body will always be ahead of the flatulent, cumbersome State.'

He was grinning. He looked like a lonely and tired man. I brought him another cup of tea. I poured myself a double whisky. He raised the cup of tea in toast to me.

'Here is to the health of Wolfclaw. May it remember the Beatitudes of Bakunin: Anarchism, Atheism and Insurrection.'

He shook my hand.

'Thank you for the tea, brother. I'll be around if you need me – in spirit if not in the flesh. They were wrong when they said I did not believe in Spirit. I believe in the Spirit of Man.'

Bakunin headed for the Ruction Room, where I watched him in animated discussion with the poet Murgan, under an enormous stuffed salmon decorated with peacock feathers.

• • • • • • • • • • • • • • • • • • •

It seemed a normal fancy dress party except that most of the people I didn't know. Killy and his wife were talking to two people I'd never seen before.

Killy introduced me. 'Michael Davitt, meet Cree Dan Macrae.'

Davitt thrust out his only arm. Davitt didn't look like a legendary Irish Land League orator.

'I was telling Fillan here that my own father came from County Mayo. He was evicted there when I was only six. That was my own introduction to the 'land question' in Ireland. My natural response was what put me in prison for 15 years from the age of 19. The Irish Land League was my monument to my own father and millions like him. I could not do otherwise. Arrest, harassment, all the same to me. A peasant's son who became a Member of Parliament. I walked out of that brothel in protest at the Boer War.'

'You knew the Highlands well.'

'I did. Speeches to three thousand men at a time, in fields, in the wind and rain. I found no difference between Highland folk and the Irish country people.'

'I was talking to Bakunin …'

'Bakunin? '

'He's here somewhere.'

'Bakunin and I must compare our prison experiences. Maybe do some arm wrestling.'

Davitt downed a whisky and I directed him to Bakunin.

'Auld Fenian bastard,' laughed Killy. 'My granda from the Sweet County Mayo used to talk about Davitt like he was God. The Mayo people thought of Davitt like that. Jesus, those old Fenians lived through prison, exile, assassination attempts. Davitt was fifteen years in prison and was rearrested practically the first week he was out. He said he lost all fear when he saw those evictions as a boy. He said those events made him so convinced of the evil of it all that he never considered the consequences of his actions. He was born at the height of the Famine – the *Starvation* he called it. He said he could only lend his oratory to Wolfclaw. Could you imagine, though, the great Land Leaguer addressing the fine people of Macqueensport?'

'He'd be in jail within a day. Things haven't changed in a hundred years.'

'Nor likely to. Anyway Dan, my other friend, Paddy Devlin.'

A small dark man stepped forward, dressed in faded tweed. His green hat was topped by an eagle feather. He shook hands with me, then began to fiddle. He leaped up on the table. The fiddling wasn't perfect, but it was wild and Devlin soon had everybody in the pub jigging and clogging away. Out of the corner of my eye, I saw the anarchist Bakunin step dancing. Davitt was waving his one arm skyward. A great roar and cheer went up when Devlin finished and sat down, grinning from ear to ear. Six pints were produced at once for the wild fiddler.

'Character, that one, Killy.'

'You don't know the half of it Dan. Devlin claims he was born in Connemara, went to Canada at fourteen on a timber ship. He went west at fifteen and was kidnapped by the Blackfeet Nation. He was about to be tortured when he started fiddling. He was spared and became a brave in the tribe, going on raids against the Shoshone and Crow. He was used as a scout, creeping up quietly on his belly. He reckons he survived because of his acute hearing.'

'Where did he come from?'

'God knows, he just walked in the door like the rest of them. Kind of disrupts our Wolfclaw business at hand. A fancy dress party. Nobody told us about the fancy dress though. It's almost like he does everything I can't do, is everything I'm not. Funny thing, his name in Blackfoot is "He Who Crawls Silently on His Belly Like the Dark Wolf." '

The Wolfclaw ranks were swelling.

• • • • • • • • • • • • • • • • • • •

Vratch was there of course. You couldn't miss her. She stood head and shoulders above the Land Leaguers, Anarchists and Blackfoot fiddlers from Connemara. Across the crowded room, her black hair was shining above her green Aran jumper. She had on faded jeans. Men hovered around her. She was always a magnet in a crowd, but seemed scarcely aware of it. She had a few female pals with her. One woman was small and muscular. She wore buckskin and moccasins. Her skin was bronzed. Her black hair pulled back tight in a ponytail.

'Isabella Gunn, of the Hudson's Bay company. I can

outfight, outwrestle, outrun anyone here, from here to hell to Hudson Bay.'

(oh fuckin shades of a Doris Day movie, it's Calamity Jane, I thought)

Isabella sprang forward, grabbed my arm, and bent it behind my neck.

'Isabella … I give … I give …'

'Son of a bitch.' She snorted. The whole pub turned to look.

An Irish voice yelled across the room.

'Pick on someone your own size, Dan.' Laughter all around.

Isabella was tensed for more trouble.

'Haud on, Isabella. Dan's OK mostly. Like you, he can speak Cree. He's small fry anyway. No match for a five foot tall Orkney woman.'

Isabella sat down in the corner. Someone brought her a drink.

Vratch told me the story.

'Isabella dressed up like a man in order to get the good wages Orkney and Shetland men got in the Hudson's Bay Company. The Company didn't employ women except to wash and iron shirts. She became an expert canoeist, voyager, guide and interpreter. The men thought she was brilliant and worked happily with her.'

'Did they discover her secret?'

'Aye, when she gave birth to a baby boy! She was shipped back to Orkney where she was teased and taunted by the locals. She was driven insane and lived in poverty until she died. She was buried in a pauper's grave. She's had poems and songs written about her all over the world, but not in Scotland.'

A useful member of the Wolfclaw?'

'Ken, a she wolf. Sorry about the rumble.'

'That's OK. I bet she *speaks* to wolves too.'

'You'll get a chance to find out.'

Vratch rejoined her group where I heard her switch into her north east-tinged Gaelic, talking to a big woman I recognized as Mairi Mhor nan Oran – Big Mary of the Songs, from Skye. She had been a great political agitator in her day, writing songs to inspire the land unrest in the Highlands and Islands. They were talking and laughing like real soul sisters, despite the great difference in their physical appearance.

• • • • • • • • • • • • • • • • • •

Conger was there too, talking to two men at a table.

'Mind if I join you Conger?'

'Nah, nah, sit down here. Dan Macrae, this is John Murdoch and Donald Macleod. Murdoch – Murchadh na Feilidh – bearded and kilted. Murdoch told us of his old campaigns in the crofting townships, where the men were afraid to attend his speeches in case the landlords and factors saw them and dismissed or evicted them. He said he had to give speeches at the sheep fanks where the men couldn't get away.

'That vicious land system kept them in serfdom on their own land,'

said John Murdoch, marvellous in full flight – a bearded prophet.

Donald 'Gloomy Memories' Macleod, sitting right here after vanishing into Canada, his death and burial virtually unrecorded. I couldn't catch much of the Gaelic, nor could Conger. I do remember one line from Murdoch.

'I taught them nothing. I tried only to awaken in them things they already knew for themselves.'

Macleod was a smaller man. He searched his glass.

'I was born again when I stopped being afraid. My anger at the Strathnaver Clearances kept me going, even in Canada where nobody would listen to me.'

I shook hands and left them talking. There was a

man at the bar I recognized immediately. His portrait had adorned every history book of the Canadian West. I tried Cree first, then French. He was smoking a big spliff.

I was surprised when he replied in English.

'*Mon père*, me, Louis Riel, a halfbreed, going to Montreal to be a priest? Everything I ever did I had to do for my people. A plaything of what had to be. Imagine fighting two tigers at once – Hudson's Bay company and the Canadian government. All I wanted was rights for my own people – the Metis. We were proud of our mixed blood, the best of both worlds we said. White and red. Old and new. French and Indian. They called 1870 a *Rebellion*. It was a Freedom Fight. When I fled to Montana, I'd had enough. I had agents on my tail, police and detectives. They drove me insane, then mocked my mental illness.'

Riel was sucking on a massive spliff which looked more like a cigar. His hands sliced the air.

'The great rebel Louis Riel, hero to thousands, confined in Quebecois insane asylums. What fun they had with that. I went to live quietly, teaching school in Montana, when my own people called me back for the last time. We would use peaceful methods this time, uniting white and red as westerners, against the exploitation by eastern bankers and profiteers. But peace never worked. It never does. So war it had to be.'

I told him briefly about Wolfclaw.

He snorted, nearly choking on his joint.

'You are a bunch of pussies. Piss ants. *Merde*, peaceful symbolists. You'll be sorry. The reply of the State to peace is *never* peaceful!'

He leapt up, spilling two pints.

'I'll show you where peace gets you, half-blood!

He ripped open his cotton shirt and showed me thick purple scars, like a swollen zipper around his neck.

'Rope burns, from my execution in 1885! Remember these scars, brother, when you think of peace!'

He went silent, into a trance. Louis Riel was said to be insane when he was tried and hung for High Treason against the Crown on a cold day at the Mounted Police barracks in Regina, Saskatchewan. The year my own grandfather was born.

• • • • • • • • • • • • • • • • • •

The night wore on. I stood back from the scene. Smoke, laughter, dim lights, fiddling, shouting, laughing, singing. My mates all there. Wolfclaw. And Lord have mercy! Bakunin, John Murdoch, Michael Davitt – my heroes. I swear too I saw other old Fenians and Land Leaguers mingling with Emma Goldman, Crazy Horse, Duncan Ban MacIntyre, Robert Johnson the blues singer and more. All there. Almost a living history of my own mental development. Hugh MacDiarmid was propped up against the bar, talking to Isaac Babel, God knows in what language!

In all that confusion and excitement, I thought of the cover of the *Sergeant Pepper* Album all those famous people, living and dead. My camera would do it. I took photos from the Ruction Room, from behind the bar, from the front door. I shot at least three films.

Many weeks later, the films came back from development. There were *no* people in them – only the bare pub, in poor light!

Beware, there is a plant growing along a Manitoba road!

• • • • • • • • • • • • • • • • • •

Chronicles. As Doctor John would say 'Such a night!' But that night didn't end with Louis Riel's public revelation of his neck scars. Just after that, a man came in the back door. He was dressed in thick tweed the colour of rust. His face was ruddy. He had bushy eyebrows.

'Ee dark drink son.'

I poured him a pint of export. I thought his accent had a blend of east coast and north Highland.

'Are you local?' I asked.

His whole face changed, darkened.

'I am and I'm not. The place is named for me after all. I'm Macqueen, gamekeeper to Mackintosh of Mackintosh.'

'The slayer of the last wolf in Scotland, on the Findhorn, in 1743.'

'Eh, so they say. Another glass please.'

He downed it quickly.

'They speak shite though. Mackintosh was an impatient man. This *black beast* had supposedly killed two children so Mackintosh wanted it hunted down. I had other things to do that day but Mackintosh was a persistent bastard and my job was on the line. The children who were supposedly killed were playing happily in the village at the time. Rumours and lies. Wolves are difficult to track because they are so canny and cowardly. They hide. They double their tracks. It was getting dark. I could imagine Mackintosh swearing, dancing his dance, cursing me for laziness. Another glass, bartender.'

He took his time with this one.

'My hounds finally backed the wolf and I "buckled wi him, dirkit him and syne whuttled his craig, and brought awa his countenance". I took the head back to Mackintosh who was fuming and swearing, claiming I'd gone on the drink instead of pursuing the black beast.'

'That's clearly the story as we've all heard it told.'

'*That* story is all true.'

'The last wolf in Scotland?'

'Another pint for the road, publican?'

I drew his pint and then handed him a bottle of malt whisky.

'With our compliments – all of us in Macqueensport.'

He held the pint up and stuck the bottle in the inner pocket of his tweed jacket. He stood up straight.

'Yes, Mr Macrae. I killed a wolf. I saw the female and four cubs in the den. The male was only trying to lead me away from his brood. I killed the sixth-to-the last wolf in Scotland. Not so impressive is it? I kept away from the place after that. I claimed the last wolf to keep people off my back. A charaid, le durachdan. Tapadh leibh!'

He walked out into the night.

He left just before I took the photographs.

That night, the Wolfclaw recruited nothing – and everything.

Chapter sixteen
NORTH WEST PASSAGE

A few days later when my head was my own again, I got a phone call from old Ben Angi vhic Ba Ba.

'Daniel, is it you?'

'Yes, it is me and nobody else.'

'Can you come right over?'

'I'll be there in a minute.'

The secrecy and urgency in her voice meant I couldn't simply ignore my eighty-eight-year-old great-aunt. I walked out the pub and down the shore road. Ben Angi's house was a white scallop shell against the dark hills. She came to the door. Four feet tall with red cheeks veined like an Ordnance Survey Map.

'Come in, come in!'

I was taken to the chair in front of the fire and given a hot sugared tea. (Angi never asked if a person took sugar – you were always given it anyway.) Angi's mantelpiece and sideboard were groaning with china cats and dogs and oriental jugs and vases, brought back by her merchant navy husband. She had a fondness for ivory scrimshaw which also covered the shelves.

I sat back comfortably, Angi in the soft chair opposite.

'Where was it now, you were, in the Canadas?'

(Oh yeah, Ben Angi always talked about 'the Canadas' – her folk memory going way back to Upper Canada and Lower Canada which later became Quebec and Ontario, hence the 'two Canadas'.)

'Winnipeg, Manitoba.'

'So, it was.' She brightened at the news. She came back with a shoebox filled with photographs and papers.

'My grand-daughter has just bought an old house

in Toronto. It was an old boarding house and she found these things.'

Ben Angi singled out a few yellow items. They were old maps, written in purple ink. The ink had only slightly blurred. It was a jagged coastline, with tiny notes written all around the margins.

Ben Angi brought a magnifying glass and pointed to the centre of the map. It said:

'East meets West Here.' (It didn't help that the map actually looked like Ben Angi's face, wrinkled and lined.) There were probably a dozen of the maps, each about the size of a pound note. They were numbered but there were some duplicates.

'But that's not why I brought you here. Look at the initials. In a tiny monogram in the lower left corner JFM.'

She raised the magnifying glass. 'It's John Farquhar surely!'

It surely was. The name meant a lot to both of us. To Ben Angi, it was a distant relative, part of her own great Highland diaspora and kinship. To me, his was the mystery and tragedy of any dreamer caught between two worlds.

• • • • • • • • • • • • • • • • • • •

John Farquhar Macrae was a local boy early last century who began to spit blood in his teens. Terminal TB – the consumption. He was offered the slight hope that cold Canadian air might heal the lesions in his lungs. He had no hope anyway, so he shipped out to Montreal with the Hudson's Bay Company and was last heard of working along the Bay itself. His family heard nothing from him for a few more years, not unusual in those days of poor communication. It was also possible John's parents did not know how to read or write, certainly in English anyway. We next hear of John Farquhar Macrae leading parties of voyageurs into the interior, trading with the Indians and trapping beaver. He was a full trader now, doing much exploration along the Arctic Circle. It seems he was given a free rein because he did a lot of work among the Cree, Assiniboine, Ojibway and Metis. He spent a few winters on the Great Slave Lake and the Athabasca.

The next part of his story is critical. John Farquhar Macrae was found dead in a cabin in northern Manitoba with a bullet in his head. The bullet came from his own gun. Nothing in the cabin was disturbed. Food, money and powder were all left alone. His traps were untouched. It could only be suicide so he was buried in a pauper's grave in unconsecrated ground along the Red River of the north. His parents tried to persuade the local parish minister in Macqueensport to allow a burial with proper gravestone in the local kirkyard. The minister did not allow church burial because of the suicide.

'He shall never be buried in consecrated ground. His self-destruction was murder, thus an affront to God.'

His parents died. That was the end of the matter. Yet, rumours began to filter back. *John Farquhar was murdered for his maps, for his secrets. He had found the fabled North West Passage years before Simpson and Amundsen. He had been silenced by power-hungry Bay Company officials who feared the impact of his discovery linking the Pacific with the Atlantic.* The most persistent rumour however, was that this famous Macqueensport son was *not* a suicide.

The story had always fascinated me. As a Macqueensport man himself, my father knew all the details of the story. He himself was a great one for conspiracies and believed Macrae had been murdered under orders from Hudson's Bay company officials.

'And if there are ghosts, old John Farquhar would be one, shivering down Portage Avenue, hurling snow balls through display windows of Hudson's Bay company and Eaton's.'

Dad took me out to the 'unofficial' graveyard, right on the river, just outside the low wall of the consecrated cemetery. I remember the fascinating names I rolled off my tongue. The old gravestones had been pocked and blurred by the ice and sun, but many of the names were legible.

'Lucien Macintosh', 'Clement Du Chien', 'Pierre Macintrois', 'Hamish Three Rivers'.

Many of the older stones were toppled, the names and dates long since vanished. It was spring, patches of snow were retreating, unclenching like frozen fingers. Small pools were pecked at by hungry robins. Ice flows clashed on the grey muddy river. Geese were flying north again. There was a bare patch, slightly raised, my father picked some of the grass away.

'His grave would be just about here.'

He said this so quietly I could barely hear him above the sound of the river. He seemed faraway then and I instinctively put out my hand to bring him back. He gripped it tightly. That was my old man for you.

I went back there a few times on my own. Each time was more depressing as the cut bank of the river claimed more and more of the unconsecrated graves. Eventually, the whole grassy bank was swept away in the spring floods.

•   •   •   •   •   •   •   •   •   •   •   •   •   •   •   •   •   •

So there we were. Ben Angi bringing tea, then drams, fussing over the fire. My hair was slicked back with sweat from the heat of the fire in the small room. The scrimshaw danced like tattooed devils in the flickering light. Ben Angi was like a tiny dervish, scurrying about. Hail pelted the windows like machine gun fire. Slates chattered in the wind. Then, sometime after 3 am, I found the key.

There was a bundle of letters, mostly water-stained and illegible. Most were ledgers and accounts, in English, but the last batch contained some discoloured letters in French, interspersed with Cree and English expressions. The man writing them must have been part native. The spelling was odd, often, phonetic. It was hard going. Ben Angi's modern French Dictionary wasn't much use, since most of the French in the letters was Quebecois *Joual*, and from another century at that:

Fev. 1867
Saint Boniface
Manitoba

'My Father, the Supreme Father, forgive me, for I have sinned a cardinal sin and fully expect to go to hell for it. This is a dying confession. On the night of 27 September, 1821, I and one other man whose own conscience must answer The Maker of Thunder and Lightning, murdered Jean Fakwar Macrois. We restrained him and shot him through the head with his own gun. We took nothing of value except some of his maps and letters which have since been taken by my accomplice from whom I have heard nothing. I think he may have gone to Ontario. It was known to all of us that Jean Fakwar had discovered the exact place where the Western Ocean greets that of the East. This dying confession was made to a fellow Metis, Baptiste Coyote Macmillan in the absence of a Priest of God. May He have mercy on this wretched sinner's soul'
> *Pierre Lucien,*
> *September 16, 1867.*

I stood up, the paper shaking in my hand. Ben Angi was shining in front of the fire, sweat running down her happy wrinkled face.

The next day I made a few phone calls to cemetery officials. Ben Angi, a regular churchgoer, went to the local minister.

• • • • • • • • • • • • • • • • • • •

On a windy day in early March Conger, Ivan and his family, Vratch, Killy and many men, women and children of Macqueensport attended a short service in the local cemetery. Snow glistened on the hills. Waterfalls gushed down, frothing with snowmelt. The sky was a struggle between blue and grey. The sun grappled with hail and rain. Our local piper played his new tune:

John Farquhar's Return to Macqueensport.

I told the people the whole story as I knew it. We said a prayer of forgiveness for the murderers. I placed a small handful of rich Manitoba earth (taken from the old cemetery along the river) in a small ornate box carved by the Cree people. The headstone was made of local granite. It read.

J.F. Macrae.
1790-1821
'Where Oceans Meet'

Maybe this was all outside the scope of Wolfclaw, but just maybe it was the best thing we ever did. And the idea was the same: restoration and justice. The truth came home. *Everybody* is coming home.

Snowdrops covered the cemetery.

Chapter seventeen

The next week belonged to Vratch, with my blessing. When I saw her in her long, tight black jeans, I thought of a muscled panther. It was a March day. She was on the shore with a motley army. Women and girls with every type of fishing tackle: trout and salmon rods, spinning tackle, salt water gear, cane poles. An assortment of hampers, flasks and picnic bags.

Vratch had already told us the basics. This was the first official day of trout season, a Saturday. She didn't want any lads involved 'in case there was trouble, ken'. Vratch knew it was becoming impossible to go to a river or burn to catch a few trout for your tea. Local angling clubs had bravely managed to keep some of the river for local use but salmon and sea trout beats were now being sold to corporations and syndicates. European and North American businessmen were paying thousands of pounds for these beats. The good hill burns and pools that both Conger and Vratch knew so well from childhood were now off-limits due to grouse and deer shooting. But Vratch had an army now. Wee girls in Australian bush hats, young mums in flowery frocks pushing babies in prams. There were also lots of older local women, including Ben Angi.

There had always been a local custom at this time of year (predating modern angling seasons) when all the village women and children would go to their favourite pools, returning in early evening with their catch, which was then divided up among the old folks. Many trout were still thin after spawning and these were always returned to the pools, but all healthy fish were kept. Sea anglers would bring in their catch as well. Of late, fewer pools were available and the custom had died out several decades before. Vratch was reviving it.

I stood across the street, having a clear view. It reminded me of one of those African political demonstrations: the bright colours, laughing women, people shimmying and singing, occasionally doing impromptu dances along the street. Vratch lead the colourful parade down the shore and through the old boatyard. However, instead of going over the hill, she turned toward the estate. Conger and I fell in line at the back of the procession. We both knew there would be trouble from the estate, now owned by Lady and Sir Frothing-Naymooth. The estate supported no workers now, but in fishing season, Daimlers and Rolls-Royces were regularly seen, transporting an assortment of upper class twits, chinless wonders and debutantes straight off the pages of the glossy country magazines. The estate centred around the loch which was connected to a staircase of pools where salmon and sea trout had spawned for centuries. It was rumoured that the estate had actually used 'electrical' fishing to rid the streams of indigenous brown trout in the belief that the predatory brownies were eating too many salmon eggs. Conger had observed wryly that these same people were on various wildlife committees to save tigers and pandas in far away lands while practising genocide on our oldest native fish.

Vratch's procession moved away slowly. She took the path over the fence stile to where the River Liabag widened as an estuary at a point where the spring tides ended. It reminded me of a baptism. There was Vratch, a tall dark shadow against the dark hills. She gave a hand signal, like an orchestra conductor, and all the people spaced themselves evenly and began fishing quietly. A few trout and sea trout were taken immediately and these were gently released, each angler carefully wetting her hands before touching the fish. Many of the fish were still thin from winter spawning. Conger noticed many of the women were fishing with barbless hooks, so the fish could be released unharmed. 'They're not taking any chances,' he said. Ben

Angi vhic Ba Ba was sitting on the grassy bank, singing in
Gaelic:

> *The land is Thine,*
> *The hills are not thine.*
> *The fish are Thine,*
> *not thine or mine.*

> *Peace to the hills,*
> *rise trout of the loch,*
> *red-belly of the deep pool,*
> *leap, Bradan,*
> *Peace to the river and all on its banks.*

It was biblical, man! Vratch was fishing upstream, with
different gear entirely. It was a fair, a carnival. Fishing was an
excuse for being in a forbidden place, excitement at the
danger to come.

Conger and I saw the dust rise from the road,
maybe a few seconds before anyone else noticed it. It rose
over the hills and birch forests, rising along the river like
steam from a steam train.

The silence was broken by the steady sound of
fishing reels being reeled in. Each woman and child set her
rod on the grass, only Vratch remained fishing. We could now
see the Land-Rover clearly as it stopped along the grassy
bank. Two men jumped out. One I recognized right away as
the local Water Bailiff. I knew him as Johnny Badger. I could
hardly believe the other man. Tall, florid, he was dressed in a
thick heather mixture tweed, green wellies, wax jacket. He
had a huge handlebar moustache. '*The Colonel*' someone
whispered. Ah, *that* Colonel. Colonel Urinal we called him,
from the time someone saw him taking a piss behind the
public toilets which he complained were too filthy for his
own use. He squelched up to Vratch. He was livid. He was
shorter than Vratch, but moved up the bank so he could

manage to look down at her. Vratch carried on fishing. 'Young lady, are you in charge of this outrage? Answer me right now or you will have to answer to the police.'

Vratch didn't even look at him. She watched the length of her fishing line, retrieving the lure slowly. The Colonel stepped forward, barely a foot from her back. Conger and I knew this was the moment. We could only see the ruddy purple of the Colonel's face.

'You sneaky ... you sneaky cunt, you will answer my question. WHO THE HELL ARE YOU AND WHAT ARE YOU DOING HERE!'

Vratch was reeling in her line furiously, not at his insistence but to retrieve the fine fish on the end of it.

'Aye, a bonny Leobag, a *plashie-dubh.*'

She unhooked the flounder and gently, casually, handed it to the Colonel. The world stopped then. I could hear the choral intake of breath. I could hear birds singing, I could hear the sift of the burn over the rocks. He flung it like a frisbee back into the estuary.

Vratch spoke, firmly.

'Aye richt, your name sir, address and date of birth. Ah already ken your registration number. Have you an Exclusion Order for these waters?'

'A *what*?' shouted The Colonel.

'Nae matter. An Exclusion Order doesn't prevent the people of Scotland from fishing estuaries up to the ordinary spring tides as marked on an Ordnance Survey Map ...'

'You Scotch bitch ...'

'Tut Colonel, the *best* kind of bitch'

'Bailiff, confiscate her rod.'

But Johnny Badger stood his ground and moved away, as Vratch cast her line.

'Colonel, these bonnie flounders are not, under recent Scottish law, classed as fresh water fish, therefore no Exclusion Order could apply in any case. Div ye ken i plashie-dubh?'

The Colonel stood to the side. His bailiff grinned stupidly. The women and girls laughed. Vratch turned to the Colonel.

'Aye, Colonel, I prefer the lugworm. Make sure the silver spoon doesn't tangle with the lang hook. Try keep the spoon near the bed. The flounder moves for the spoon, then sees the lugworm in its wake. My people have fished for flounder for centuries this way. Fancy a twirl?'

The Colonel spluttered again. He shook like a man in an invisible strait jacket. His eyes appealed to the bailiff, who looked to his feet, pawing at the ground with the heel of his wellies.

'So Colonel, no Exclusion Order and legal fishing up to the normal spring tide for flounders and other estuarine fish. Look up the law. I'm tempted also to do a citizen's arrest for harassment. Plenty witnesses. Instead, I'll probably report you to the police for attempting to subvert the ancient rights of the common fowk of Scotland. By the way, the public toilets are pristine. Most of us have learned to use them by now. If ye need ony lessons, let me know, ken.'

The Colonel slumped to the safety of his Landrover, while the crowd cheered and laughed. We watched the dust cloud disappear over the horizon. The colour of the crowd was a huge quilt under the sky and from where Conger and I stood, we could both see Vratch's grin on the reflection of the river. It moved and danced over the water surface. The women and children began to fish again. Vratch piled her flounders up like a stack of pancakes.

It was pure Vratch. Composure, cheekiness, fact and perfect timing.

As it grew darker, we joined the cavalcade as its colours surged down the grey track, all under a darkening mackerel sky. In between the talk, the singing and laughing, we heard thrushes singing.

Chronicles: *Vratch went out today to win. She had her facts, her wit, her composure. She did all of this with support, but the courage was hers alone. The Colonel was a foul, impetuous man and could have done anything. Vratch took a chance and won.*

I thought a long time ago of something my mother rarely spoke about. It was not about her own people but of people further north. The Shaking Tent. A small tent retreat, on the axis of some phenomenal power connecting the stars to the centre of the earth. The person going to the tent had to win something for the people or tribe, at great risk to his or her mental health. The tent spun and shook, strange voices and shouts were heard. Nothing would ever be the same for the person. But a lost child would be found. A missing body recovered. A sickness or plague abated. Like any healing, the healer could be diseased, crippled or afflicted in some way, as payment for the good luck of the tribe or people. All of this is something I can't say more about because it is not of my people, or my experience. And I believe it is sacred, for those with the right knowledge only.

Seeing Vratch laughing, a bag of flounders slung over her shoulder, I could see no affliction or retribution, just courage, pure and distilled, perfect, under a setting sun. Her Shaking Tent left everybody healed.

Chapter eighteen

And that was maybe Wolfclaw's finest hour, its apogee, when Vratch and her rainbow army sent 'downpresser man' packing.

'*Hey downpresser man, where you gonna run to?*'

It was never to get as good again. Our next meeting in late March brought home the point that our time was running out. Factors, landlords, police, lairds – all scurrying around taking notes, phoning, shitting themselves, maybe, but my own encounter with them left me with no illusions. We could howl a few times more before they picked us off one by one, and a wolfpack only exists as a *pack*. It was a cold March night in the Haddock Arms. We put a brave face on it.

'Three cheers for Vratch!'

Vratch's whole body grinned.

'Tae the Wolfclaw, ken!'

The Wolfclaw, we all *ken*. Then, I told them the truth. 'I was questioned by a man the other day. A CID *wolf hunter*. The posse is closing in. They don't know *what* but they sure as hell know *who*.'

I could hear a collective sigh.

Killy wiped his hand through his dark hair.

'I thought I was the only one. Nothing major, but they've been asking about my tax status, Irish connections, meaning IRA connections, my self-employment. All letters. A few innuendoes about my reasons for being in this country. I didn't bring the letters. I haven't told my wife yet, either. I can't sleep at night, not usual for me.'

Killy pushed away his pint. His bravery wasn't convincing. For a start, Killy's natural face was always a grin-cum-laugh. He wasn't fooling any of us. Vratch saw it too.

'Ah ken, Killy. Mah ain public exhibition wull add me tae their list. Ah've haird nuthin at work. Some smirkin. That fish-in was mah comin oot, mah debutante ball. Thi

Plashie-dubh Princess, thi Flounder Quine.'

Vratch, bless her, was still smiling. She tossed her curls and raised her pint in mock toast.

Conger growled from his table.

'Finished before we started. They're also stepping up pressure about the island. I think I can hang on to it forever , but this steady drizzle of forms, public enquiries and regulations is wearing us all down. 'A scarecrow in a hailstorm' is what my old man said. No coincidence if you ask me. Don't get me wrong. I think we've shaken up a few people and I've felt better than I ever have. The whole overseas land-reclaiming project has really taken off. And that is a legal struggle we'll win. Potent, man, potent. My folks and I would fight on legally in any case. But we've had fun. We've created something that won't die.'

Then Ivan came in, eyes down. He handed me a letter.

Dear Mr. Volk,

You will remember in our original proceedings that you were awarded only a conditional asylum in the UK for you and your family. The conditions were clearly spelled out. One of those conditions was that you shall not engage in any illegal acts. It has come to our attention that you may be peripherally involved in malicious damage to property and other acts against public amenity. Bear in mind any conviction could result in termination of your conditional asylum and result in extradition. However, further information about other individuals who may also be involved may be seen in your favour. We have enclosed a Russian translation for your convenience. Perhaps we will be hearing from you.

Yours sincerely,

A.T.K.
For H.M.

I held the letter but Ivan kept his hand on it, the paper shaking because he was shaking with rage himself. Killy put a double vodka in front of Ivan. Ivan downed it, then began shouting:

'Those dog-fucking, shit-eating sons of whores, those ulcerous Imperial arse-licking borsch boilers, those filthy penis-stroking vodka-poisoning apparatchiks …'

I put my arm around Ivan.

'Calm down, Comrade, this is just some heat to test us. We're all under pressure but we'll make it … we'll make it.'

I knew it was a lie. Ivan was in serious trouble.

'Ivan, man, don't tell your wife and daughter just yet. Besides, you can leave all this now. We'll be winding down anyway.'

Ivan pulled free.

'I can't hear of this. Shall I prove my loyalty to the Wolfclaw?'

NO we all shouted in unison! That broke the tension and Ivan sat down with the rest of us, all four viewing that clarity as we would a crystal ball.

'Well ma loons, fa's next?'

Conger grunted.

'I reckon the wolf needs to howl just the once more, as a parting shot, as a wolf pissing on the hunter's trouser leg.'

'May as well, can't dance' muttered Killy through his pint.

I agreed with Conger but identified with Killy's tiredness.

'Count me in,' thundered Ivan, spilling all the drinks on the table – dark Guinness mingling with clear vodka,with light lager washing into it all.

'Any ideas?'

Vratch was right in there.

'Aye, Rocky. Fuckin aye, Rocky, ken?'

Conger leapt up. 'Aye, aye, ROCKY.'

Killy said he didn't know who Rocky was. Ivan looked puzzled. It was a natural way to bow out, full of symbolism, highly visible and would send a few shock waves throughout Scotland. Maybe further, too.

• • • • • • • • • • • • • • • • • •

Rocky was a near life-size statue standing on a granite pedestal in a clump of bracken on a sea-cliff just around the village headland. Its stone was so clarted, faded and wind-pocked that it looked more like a standing stone than the model of Macqueen it was said to represent. Nobody knew that for certain. Rocky was some kind of huntsman or gamekeeper, rifle pointed, eyes intent on something on the horizon – no doubt a slinking wolf. The statue had been commissioned and paid for by a local estate owner, over a hundred years ago; whose own London family had been involved in slavery in the previous century and had become wealthy from it. The landowner's descendants had no connection to the area, having sold the estate at vast profit. Some of the family once had serious flirtations with Nazism before World War II. Some photographs were produced, showing picnics with Hitler and Goering. Some say leading Nazis had even enjoyed stag hunting not far where Rocky now stood. Rocky was seen as a bit of a joke and most local folk despised his builder and his descendants. This lump of rain-riddled granite had touched many lives over the years: stalkers, rock climbers, shepherds, estate workers. Some still decorated him with condoms, bras, old scarves. Someone once dressed him up in some costly lingerie, later reported missing from a kirk elder's wife. Rocky was in turn resented, tolerated, ignored and sentimentalized. But he stood, through wind and rain, gales and snow. Rocky bided, thrawn. Stags rubbed their rank sex on him. Stonechats shat on him. Dogs pissed on him. Rumours abounded about Rocky's security: laser beams, electrical alarms, automatic lights.

'Bollocks,' said Conger. 'Rumours put out by Rocky's hyphenated erectors.'

Vratch was no fan of Rocky. 'Onywye, Rocky was put up by a slaver and maintained by Nazis and mebbe represents a mannie who didna kill thi last wolf ataa, ken. Fa saiz there isnae wolves in Scotland?'

I intervened. 'What do we do then? Decorate him? Graffiti?'

Killy was more certain.

'Explode him. Rocky to smithereens.'

'No', said Conger, 'that'll be bad blood. We need to use him to make a point and maybe win some public support too.'

Ivan was growling at all this, baring his forearm. Ivan was all for hammering Rocky into dust.

So, the Wolfclaw majority was all for destruction, but Conger's opinion was probably closest to local opinion. I had another idea.

'We could replace him. Keep him safe. Give him a new home and get something more appropriate for the millennium. Let's suppose Rocky is meant to be Macqueen who may not have killed the last wolf and wasn't keen on the job anyway.'

'Paper, pencil, anyone?' Vratch asked.

Killy handed her both.

Vratch leaned over the paper, curls forming a veil over it. She scrawled, while chewing the end of the pencil. She put her finished work in the centre of the table.

ROCKY AFORE: (Rocky points his gun at something on the horizon.)

ROCKY EFTER: (Rocky's gun is missing, he holds his empty arms in a cradling position.)

ROCKY RESTORED: (Rocky has a wolf cub in his arms!)

'What's he holdin, Vratch, his messages, or a carry-oot from the Haddock Arms?'

'Na, a wolf, ken. A baby wolf, he's feedin wi a bottle!'

We all laughed but could see the sense of her plan.

'We spirit Rocky awa for surgery, ken, a wee bittie sculptural surgery. Restoration. We'll clean the stone. No destruction or vandalism. We'll win some public support. Add a few wee flourishes.'

I was still thinking of Ivan. 'Remember the movie about the battle of the Alamo where they draw a line in the sand with a sabre and invite anyone who wants to leave to step over the line? See that dark floorboard? Anyone who doesn't want to *do* Rocky can step over the dark board, no questions asked. Ivan, you especially.' I joined the rest on the other side. Nobody moved. We stared at the dark floorboard, slightly warped, almost a shadow to the lighter board next to it. We stared and stared. OK. We all stood together, just like at the Alamo. Rocky it is ... the last howl of the wolf.

Chronicles

Memorial to any human being. Poem, story, song, photograph. Sum total of actions, thoughts, feelings, offspring. Memorials: wood, stone, marble, granite. Statues: to imperialists, slave owners, serial killers, hustlers, fraudsters, war criminals, memorials of one class to another – in preposterous times and places. I remember that Polish man in South Dakota who was appalled at the monstrous creation on Mount Rushmore. With his son was going to redress the balance by blasting and carving a statue of Crazy Horse. He thought it would take three or four generations to finish. Heroes? They all came tumbling down all over the eastern bloc, pulled down by people, attacked with sledge hammers, jack hammers, stone drills and dynamite. Some carted off for safe-keeping to museums and barns, sold to private collections, sold for food on the black market, these pigeon-shitted commissars, bureaucrats, black marketeers. Pulverize them for garden chippings, landfill, use for flood control, ideal for drainage, give them back to the people they oppressed in the first place.

• • • • • • • • • • • • • • • • • • •

The discoverers who 'discovered' and named places discovered and named thousands of years previously; names borrowed from politicians, merchants, queens and kings and given to places already well-named by native peoples with maps in their heads. Ojibway names, Cree names, Assiniboine names, and of course, Gaelic names; statues imposed on a people's songs, poems and stories, and no need for faith in marble and sandstone, the prerogative of people who would fawn and grovel in the face of arrogance, gluttony and greed. Maybe all this is good. A memorial in reverse. This is what arrogance looks like. Beware. But *not* Rocky. Built by a slaver maybe, but Rocky himself was a working man sent out to do a distasteful job. He did it. That's all. Like Atlas, holding up the town. Rocky could benefit from a walkabout, a blow out, a dram. I thought back to that strange night in the Haddock Arms. In imagination or hallucination, I met the man – the wolf-slayer – who was not suited to that kind of memorial, nor bearing the least resemblance to our stone man on the hill.

Rocky, *a ghradh*, explosives, acid, jack hammers, sledge hammers. And suppose, just suppose, somewhere in the Cairngorms or along the Great Glen, a she-wolf may be suckling her whelps at this very moment. We can't know, so the monument may be a memorial to a monstrous lie, to arrogance and ignorance, just like many another statue. Given the later family history, a monument to genocide might have said more about their values than anything else, yet wolves never murdered their own kind.

• • • • • • • • • • • • • • • • • •

I looked out the small window in the topmost room of the Haddock Arms and I saw a comet coming into view, one appearing every four thousand years. It was brightest in that night sky, sparking its way to the outer fringes of the solar system, to ride the rim of Pluto. A white powder smudge point, a fingerprint in the sky. Speeding away from this sad beautiful planet (a good idea) fire and ice, gliskin through the heavens. A waking comet dreaming over the haze of Macqueensport. Dreaming of statues toppling in the cities and country, tumbling down ravines and gullies, into deep pools and lochans, pedestals of sparkling granite or sombre sandstone left as tombstones or memorials to women and children, to men with no living or remembered memorial. Some statues deserve to stay: to soldiers, servants, men and women of the people: not admirals, generals, kings or queens; pedestals and statues cleaned, enhanced; resting places for birds and butterflies, trellis for flowers and vines until finally claimed by bracken and heather, silent as the people who had no voice and required no memorials other than their brief time on the land.

Chapter nineteen

A wolf pack is the sum total of all intelligence, cunning and physical strength. Our sum total agreed that Rocky was an object of restoration, not destruction. One of Rocky's extraordinary qualities was his human scale: exactly man-size on a pedestal the height and size of an upturned fish box. A more haughty or imposing statue wouldn't have been spared by anyone having a local connection. As a person, this Stone Man was pretty lean, with huge gaps between his oxters and legs. Ivan reckoned he could carry him a short distance at least, judging from our description. Individually, we all went to have a look.

Vratch: Aha mannie, nae even mah heicht. How heavy, ava? Ah'll dae some calculations. A slight gamekeeper nae typical o a Nazi-inspired chiel. Let's see: bolted oan i pedestal, cemented oan, or baith? Ah'd crack him alang baith feet, careful nae tae crack his kweets, expose ony bolts, cut thur heids aff an cowp him gently oan i bracken. Twa choices then, ower i steep cliff wi a rope or doon i gentler slope. Ane wey instant, depends oan wind an sea, i ither longer, less risk tae Rocky bit mair tae us. Ane chiel tae keep watch, ane tae cut, twa tae puil, ane keepin guard. If by sea, twa in i boatie, twa on i rope, ane oan guard. Aye, an a deeper pairt o me thinks i statue is wrang-heidit. I mannie's speirin fur a wolfie, he kens thur is ane still oot there. *Ah ken it tae.*

• • • • • • • • • • • • • • • • • •

Killy: blow the fuckin thing I say. A statue here among the most ancient rock on earth, mountains millions of years old. Only a slaver or Nazi could do it. Sorry Rocky but. Save a lot of trouble. Remote control. Maybe mount some fireworks nearby to add to the occasion. Public holiday, broad daylight. Good chippings for a garden path, glistening in the rain, shining under moon and sun. In time the pedestal would become a rounded boulder like any other. However, we'd become the villains, destroying a landmark built by a slaver whose descendants flirted with fascism, yet only the Scots could cluck and coo so over a dead stone man.

'A nation of black-mouth necrophiliacs,' hissed my uncle. 'Scots find it easier to love the dead than the living, look how they treat their poets!' We'll need: a drill, a stonemason's saw (battery-powered) or a long extension lead to power it. Cut one foot free, then the other and over the cliff on rope to a waiting boat.

• • • • • • • • • • • • • • • • • •

Ivan: this is some runt. The Russians used statues to frighten us, to make us seem puny and weak. I would offer this stone man black bread and vodka. Our great stone men all came down; Lenin in the warehouse, Brezhnev broken in garages. We had our own heroes; not Russians, but ploughmen, poets, singers and our statues were poems and songs. And why are statues always to killers? This Rockboy is not happy so we will take him for a walk. I could even carry him.

• • • • • • • • • • • • • • • • • •

Conger: I'm closer to Rocky than the rest, have grown old with him, played round him as a schoolboy. We never despised the creation, only the creator; maybe that's my theology too. I can't even mind the original subscriber; some version of the same Nazi shite, whatever that was over a hundred years ago. I hope you can swim, rocky man, because over the edge you must go. I have a few ideas here.

• • • • • • • • • • • • • • • • • •

Cree Dan: the whole is equal to the sum of the parts. We need:

five people, power source, a very long extension lead, stonemason's drill, stonemason's saw, several old heater lagging sheets (protective cover), long road, boat, one sculptor with restoration idea, one replica to occupy the pedestal. Beyond requisition: good luck, mist, calm seas, soft weather. At least we were to have the last three.

• • • • • • • • • • • • • • • • • •

April Monday, sunny, calm. Ivan and I had our 'checklist'. We would have to do everything in the dark since Rocky was visible nearly everywhere from the village, not because of the height but because of his prominence on a distinctive curve of headland cliff. The usual walk up to Rocky was a few miles through a gorse and bracken moorland. The direct cliff was fenced off to provide some safety but curving a straight two hundred feet to the rocks below, affected by spring tides. Here Conger and Killy would receive the padded statue. The sea that day was calm and the hot day insured a cover of heat haze in the evening. Conger had told me a few days before that the boat was guaranteed. All our gear was in Vratch's car which she drove to the gentler more secluded side of the hill. We divided the gear up and took separate routes. I went to the workshop near the base of the hill, where I could connect the electric cable to power the drill and saw. Vratch and I knew the route better than Ivan, so arrived slightly sooner. Our hearts thumped away in the mist. I looked at my watch. 9:30 pm. The boat was to set off at 10 o'clock, to allow enough time for us to cut the statue loose, wrap it in the old lagging for protection and get it on the ropes for lowering over the cliffs. Ivan crouched near the statue.

'It can not be wired surely.'

'No, Ivan. It couldn't be,' but I was nervous as I plugged the drill in. I took it from Ivan. I would test my own instinct. I pressed the trigger. The noise broke the silence and amplified somehow in the mist. I drilled holes at the point where the feet joined the pedestal. It was slow going but I drilled several holes. I switched to the saw and sawed between the drill holes. Sweat dripped into the dust at my feet. I saw Vratch in the mist, her curls smooring the distant village at her back. In this mist, we couldn't be seen from below. The saw brought small sparks from the stone. It was ready. Vratch and I, arms overlapping, leaned into Rocky and gently rocked him ... rocked him ... rocked him ... he came free in big Ivan's arms!

'Odin, dva, tri' and Ivan lifted Rocky right off the ground. 'It is nothing, this Rocky is a featherweight.' Ivan carried the statue over to the fence at the cliff edge.

'Careful, big man, don't you go down too.' Vratch brought over the lagging and wrapped the stone man up in it, tying it firmly with twine. This would protect him on the way down. We left the statue leaning against the wire fence. I motioned Vratch over. It was only 10.20, ten minutes until the boat would signal from below. With my small torch, we found my own cache – 'Rocky Replica' a concoction of red ash, concrete and old casting clay. It was a remarkable replica, done by an old sculptor friend of mine. It was much lighter than the original. It had small countersunk holes in each foot, which received heavy masonry screws. I had a small Tupperware tub of ready-mix concrete which I filled the holes with. I'd worked on the cement at home to get a reddish colour. It wouldn't pass close inspection but it would do until Restored Rocky could assume his old place on the pedestal. I can't forget the scene. Visibility was almost nil, but I could see Ivan, monstrous against the horizon, Vratch prowling like a nervous panther, her black curls bouncing with each step. We watched the sea, until we saw the clear flash of a torch from below. The boys were there and ready. I brought a piece to clamp to the the thick metal fence post and attached a pulley to it. We ran the end of the rope through the pulley, Vratch and I took the rope back to the pedestal, where we sat with our feet planted securely against it. Ivan lifted Rocky over the fence onto the small strip of grass separating the fence from the cliff edge. Ivan then pushed the statue slowly into space, so slowly that we did feel a sharp lurch but with warning enough for Vratch and I to dig in. We were concentrating so much on holding the rope and planting our feet against the pedestal that we couldn't believe a sound arising from near the cliff. It was a low groan, almost a sigh. We thought it was Ivan straining. I could feel a nervous tremor pass through Vratch's leg which was next to mine. Our flesh crawled when Ivan whispered:

'What was that?' We heard it again, louder, more painful. We saw Ivan crowd to the cliff edge, where Rocky swung slowly in space. Ivan shone a torch to the right of the statue.

'There's a man down there!'

We managed to tie the rope off on the pedestal and crossed carefully to the edge. In Ivan's torchlight, we saw a man wedged in the rocks. He was bleeding. Ivan didn't hesitate but went right over the cliff. We saw him reach for Rocky and with a slash of his famous mackerel blade, Rocky disappeared and the rope went slack. Ivan asked for more rope so we slackened some off at the pedestal end. Ivan had begun slashing his own red shirt into ribbons, using them to stem the man's flow of blood.

Ivan shouted up. 'He's bleeding badly. We have to get him down and we don't have time to take him back up. Too much risk. We'll have to send him down. He'll probably die from his injuries anyway so we have to do it.'

Vratch and I both shouted yes and went back to the pedestal, giving slack to lower the man down to Conger and Killy, who were nervously expecting a stone man, not a wounded living one.

•   •   •   •   •   •   •   •   •   •   •   •   •   •   •   •   •

Killy: Conger and I had no trouble with the boat, both having fished her before. We arrived at 10.20 exactly and saw a white shroud hanging above our heads, Rocky on schedule. It was misty and we were both nervous about being in so close to the rocks. Conger and I weren't sure what happened next, as we didn't want to flash too much light around. Then, we saw something crash down, splitting on the rocks and vanishing into the cliff pools. We looked up but still saw something dangling in mid-air! It was being lowered down, no statue but a broken man, wrapped in pieces of what we immediately recognized as strips of Ivan's favourite shirt. At first, we thought it was Cree Dan, since it was too small for Ivan, but more stocky than Vratch and a bit shorter. But we had never seen this man before. We raced the engines for the pier where we phoned an ambulance, which came at once.

'We were setting some creels around the Point when we saw this guy fall from the cliffs. We think he was a rock climber.'

• • • • • • • • • • • • • • • • • • • •

Dan: We got the whole story later, but meanwhile, Ivan, Vratch, and myself were in a mist-shrouded dwalm. We were numb with disbelief that everything had changed through no fault of ours. Until we discovered the bleeding man, everything was going perfectly. In shock, we gathered up our gear and walked down together. Vratch put her arms over each of our shoulders and we vanished down into the mist. At midnight, as to plan, we met Conger and Killy in the pub and got the rest of the story. I set a bottle of whisky on the table in my room, and put down five glasses.

'*Slainte*, to the Wolfclaw.'

'Tae the Wolfie, mind big Ivan went over that cliff like a lemming.'

Conger spoke then 'Well Rocky, sweet dreams down below. That bit of tidal pool is too dangerous for a diver so we 'll probably never seen the original again.'

I argued that the replica might fool folk for a while anyway, until its materials were weakened by the wind and rain. That might take months, maybe a few years. 'Who was the guy?' I wondered aloud.

'Neither Conger or I got a good look but we'd never seen him before around here.'

'Ivan?'

'He wasn't dressed for hiking or rock-climbing.'

'Then what the hell was he doing up there in the mist – so late?'

I poured another round of whisky. Silence. We were all thinking the same thing. How much had he seen and heard? How did he know we'd be there? Did someone tell him? Vratch reminded me we didn't hear the groan until we'd nearly finished everything. I thought maybe he had fallen earlier but was only gaining consciousness when we came.

'Well, the ambulance was in a hurry to take him away but the police will want to question Conger and myself about our strange fishing arrangements.'

I looked at the Wolfclaw, tired beaten children. Even Vratch had no colour, her hair was matted with sweat and dust. I'd seen a resignation and vulnerability in her face that I'd never imagined possible. We all agreed we'd just have to wait and see what happened. We would try to find out more about the man in hospital. Even if he recovered he might not remember anything. He was never conscious from the time Ivan tied him until he was delivered to the ambulance. The next few days answered all of our questions.

Chronicles

I could not sleep. I took a half bottle of whisky up to my room. Amber bottle, clear head, and I had a beautiful rush of logic that often proceeds mental mayhem. Rocky is gone. The injured man either saw or heard us, or he didn't. If not, the police will still interview Conger and Killy in greater detail.

The statue may be dredged up as evidence. Can fingerprints survive salt water? Can we dredge up Rocky and restore him before his absence is noted?

The replica. If discovered, they will try to trace who made it and who placed it there. (The sculptor lives in Glasgow.) Wolfclaw Code: no individual is left on his or her own. One incarceration or interview and we will all go for the same. It all depends on a stranger who almost bled to death on a cliff edge; a stranger whose life we saved. Surely, good karma will come back to us. I fall asleep dreaming of panthers.

The bottle was empty. My head is not. Ideas cut and collide like a thousand granite shards, jagged, sharp, slicing my flesh, using my brain for a whetstone.

Chapter twenty

The national press mentioned the incident briefly:

ROCK CLIMBER INJURED
A rock climber was recovering in the local Mackenzie Hospital yesterday, having been rescued by two local fishermen below the headlands of Macqueensport. He was not named, pending notification of relatives. His condition is thought to have stabilized, after suffering several broken ribs and a punctured lung, as well as concussion.

The article gave us hope that the 'fishermen' weren't given much attention by the ambulance men on the pier. All of us hoped the injured man would recover but hoped also that he possibly didn't see or hear much of what went on that night on the hill.

Meanwhile, the Wolfpack was moping. The Haddock Arms was cleaned and recleaned; the bar sparkled. Ivan and I only went through all the motions, with a numbness bordering on paralysis. I sensed the trouble and deep thought in Ivan's face, in his furrowed brow, in his pursed lips. Vratch, Conger and Killy were setting about their work in the same way. So close but now so far away – all because of a lacerated and battered man lying in a local hospital: a man with no name.

• • • • • • • • • • • • • • • • • •

The nurse entered the hospital room. 'He's showing real improvement, doctor. He's more alert and I think he might even be speaking properly in a few days.'

'Yes. He was very lucky. He lost a lot of blood but the cold weather up there probably slowed his blood loss. I think he wants your attention, nurse.'

'Doctor, he's making writing motions. He wants a pen and paper.'

'What's he trying to write?'

'It's just a scrawl at the moment.'

'Well, nurse, I leave it to you for now. We'll give him another day or so before we bother him too much with questions. Maybe we can learn more about him meanwhile. I believe he had no identification or wallet with him. So far, nobody has been reported missing from local hotels or Bed and Breakfasts.'

The man had scribbled something on the writing pad and was pushing it towards the nurses.

D. MACRAE. HADDOCK ARMS.

That must be him – a Mr Macrae. From somewhere that looks like 'Hamilton' or 'Haddington'. We'll follow that up. Maybe it's the name of his house. He's dropped his pen. We'll assume Mr Macrae but need to verify it first before we release any information to the press.'

The nurses left the room and the man went into a deep sleep. When he awoke, the nurses saw an agitated man who had knocked his pad and pencil to the floor. The nurse retrieved it and the man with no name began writing furiously.

•　•　•　•　•　•　•　•　•　•　•　•　•　•　•　•　•　•

I answered the phone.

'Mr Macrae?'

'Speaking.'

'I wonder if you could come over to the hospital this afternoon?'

'May I ask why?'

'We have a recovering patient – an accident victim – who is asking for you.'

'Has he recovered enough to speak?'

'No ... no not yet. but he can write quite clearly now and he has written your name down. '

'Ah ... fine. I'll be over. When are visiting hours?'

'I think we can waive those for now. You'll understand when you get over here. In fact, can you come right over?'

'I'll be there in fifteen minutes.'

The hospital was about a mile out of town and in order to clear my head, I decided to walk it. The village was buzzing with tourists: German rucksackers, tour buses from the north of England: the women with identical 'cauliflower' hairstyles, husbands grumbling in front of shops. Well-dressed women stepping carefully out of new Volvos and Saabs. Many of the trees were beginning to bloom pink or white. Daffodils and crocuses covered the grass verges. Fat thrushes and blackbirds bounded over the grass for worms. As I walked out of the town, I noted the early wild primroses scattered like broken bits of moon on the wet stone cliffs. My heart was thumping wildly and I was sweating, not just due to the heat. That guy on the cliff knew me and was well enough to write down my name. Who the hell was he? How did he know my name? Was he up there that night by accident? Who lead him to me? A mole? Wire-tapping? Phone-tapping, bugging? Maybe just the usual gossip. I clenched my fists as I neared the front door of the hospital. Ivan had risked his life to save this daft bugger, whoever he might be. I was angry. I decided to go on the offensive and ask him why he was snooping on us.

Two nurses were walking past the door. I didn't recognize them. They weren't local. They guessed who I was.

'Mr Macrae?'

I nodded.

'Follow us please.'

Although it was a small cottage hospital, I'd never been in it. Down a short corridor, then a smaller wing to the left. Everyone local knew this hospital specialised in trauma: climbing and fishing accidents, broken bones and severe wounds. They took me into a room, then left as if on cue. The patient was propped up in bed. He was heavily covered in bandages. Only some of his face was visible. There was a pad and paper on the nearby table. His face was turned away from me. Then he turned. It wasn't instant recognition, but I fastened on the eyes. Staring, slate-blue. I couldn't recall his name but it was definitely the man who questioned me weeks before in the Haddock Arms. He had frightened the shit out of me then but was still formidable enough, wrapped up like a mummy. His thin mouth threatened a smile. I went over to the side of the bed where he kept his pencil and pad. A nurse reappeared with a tray.

'Tea or coffee Mr Macrae?'

'Yes ... yes please. Black coffee, no sugar.'

The nurse left. I sipped slowly. The hot coffee seemed to jerk my mind awake.

Bandage Man wrote in the pad.

'First Mr Macrae thanks for saving my life. I don't remember much about the whole thing.'

The nurse returned with a pad and paper for me.

'Why do you think it was me who saved you?'

'You – I mean "You" collectively.'

(Shit. He was still very capable of playing mind games despite being wrapped up in hospital bandages with his tongue swollen in his mouth.)

'How do you know I was even up there?'

'I remembered your voice. There were three of you up there. Three different voices. One foreign – maybe eastern bloc; one woman with a north-east accent.'

(Nothing wrong with this man, nurse. Ready to be discharged.)

'How do you think you got to the hospital?'

'I was told two fishermen brought me.'

'It was they who saved your life?'

'Yes, but I don't think they were really fishermen. I think they were there for the same reasons you three were. Fishermen wouldn't be out around dangerous cliffs on such a foggy night. But that is another investigation Mr. Macrae.'

I gulped the coffee, letting it linger on my tongue, burning. My tongue, *Cut it out.*

'Shouldn't we save those questions until you are better?'

'Perhaps.'

I took a risk. 'What do you think we were all doing up that hill?'

He paused, pencil in air.

'Destruction of the statue.'

'Why?'

'Symbolic, political reasons. But you didn't succeed because sources tell me it's still up there. My accident was poor timing for you. I guess it prevented you from finishing your scheme. I don't remember much of anything else though.'

I spluttered some of my coffee down my shirt.

'You *don't* remember much else?'

He now seemed very tired and I almost felt sorry for him. I moved to go.

'Nurse?'

She came at once.

'I'd like to continue when the patient is rested. It must be a strain for him.' (It was I who was sweating.)

Then, the patient grabbed my shirt with his left hand and began scribbling with his right.

'Macrae, I do not know it all but I know enough to put *you* away at least.'

I pulled away. He wrote again.

'Or even better, the big Russian.'

I grabbed my own writing pad again.

'What do you want me to do ? Why did you call me to the hospital?'

'Stop. Just all of you stop what you are doing. Up to now, these are merely acts of vandalism but they may have wider political consequences. Just stop.'

'I am just an individual. I can't make decisions for any others.'

'Mr Macrae. I have a fair idea who they are. And I am certainly able to find out. I am grateful to you for saving my life and that might well have been a team effort. The deal is simple. You stop this secret-society vandalism mumbo-jumbo and I will stop my investigation. A life for a life. Simple. Please think about it.'

'I will at least think about it.'

'Good. I will be here for a week or so at least so you have that long to consult your colleagues. And thanks for not bringing me fruit or chocolates. I never eat the stuff.'

(Christ – more humour from Mr Slate eyes. He still never told me his name and clearly wasn't going to.)

The nurses came back.

'Thank you for coming,' they chirped.

'Sure. I'll be back.'

• • • • • • • • • • • • • • • • •

Out of the dark into the light. From enclosure to freedom. Birds in the sky. Flowers on the hill, a few optimistic butterflies blowing like flower petals. The Wolfclaw had just become extinct as sure as the last wolf. It had been hunted down by a mummie with no name; its death warrant had been signed on cheap hospital stationery. But I felt like I had just put down a bag of coal, or heavy rucksack. I felt free of a great burden. I would have to see the others at once. Being followed? No. Anyway, who cares now?

Killy didn't live that far away and I headed up his road. I walked for a few minutes, then saw his van coming down the hill. He rolled down the window.

'Jump in, Dan, I'm off to the tree nursery. You look

like you've seen the Bogeyman himself.'

'I have done. I've just been to the hospital to see the man whose life you saved ...'

Killy jerked the van over into a layby.

'Let's hear this, brother. That mystery man has kept me awake for days.'

'The man in the hospital never told me his name but I know who he is. He's the same CID man who interrogated me in the pub that day. He knows a lot about all of us.'

'Did he say anything?'

'He can't speak yet. His tongue was badly damaged in the fall. He writes everything on paper. He wants us to call the whole thing off. Our life for his. He just wants to stop. A bogey. A draw.'

Killy drew symbols on the dashboard dust.

'What did you tell him?'

'I said I'd have to think about it. I told him I'd have to talk it over with a few "colleagues".'

'Can you call his bluff? Find out how much he really knows? Does he know who rescued him at sea?'

'No, he'd been unconscious by then. He knows Ivan, me and Vratch. He also told me he doesn't remember the boat but he said he didn't believe the two men in the boat were really fishermen.'

'Shite. Can we just change tactics?'

'No Killy. I think he's got us. He would still track us individually. I think up to now he's willing to see it as youthful vandalism. Conceited pranks. And there's Ivan too.'

'The big man. The big Russian really saved the guy's life. Would he leave Ivan alone?'

'He said he would leave us *all* alone if we stopped.'

'Then Dan, we should stop – not for good – just lie fallow for a while, for Ivan's sake.'

'Right Killy. That's my feeling too. I'll tell CID it's a deal.'

'Wasn't it de Valera said a treaty signed under force was morally invalid?'

'De Valera would say that, but can you drop me off at Vratch's?'

'Right bhoy, and thanks for letting me know so soon.'

• • • • • • • • • • • • • • • • • • •

The pier was abuzz with tourists eating ice cream cones, queuing up for sightseeing boats. East Coast trawlers lined the pier, great eastern bloc factory ships floated further beyond. I walked to a quiet corner of the pier. I saw Vratch sitting on a pile of fish boxes. She was eating an apple. She waved in a windscreen wiper motion. I went over.

'Fit like Dan? Want a bite?'

'Sorry, Eve, not today anyway. I think we were finally kicked out of the Garden today. I've just been up to the hospital talking to our man with no name – our mystery man on the hill.'

Vratch paused, apple mid-air, then chucked it into the sea where it was attacked by seagulls. Her eyebrows asked the question.

'It turned out to be the same CID man who questioned me in the pub some weeks ago. We may as well call him Smith since he has never told me his name.'

'Talking too?'

'No Vratch, he couldn't speak but we talked on paper. Bottom line is, he wants a deal. We saved his life. He'll save ours by dropping his investigation if we stop what he called vandalism.'

'How much does he know?'

'Too much Vratch, too much. Killy thinks we should lie fallow, agree to stop, maybe change directions. It's really Ivan we're worried about. They're definitely on to him. Smith has done his homework well. I decided to speak to each of you before I go back to the hospital to give him our answer. What do you think I should tell him?'

'Dan, we all ken we're near the end of the road on this. I agree we should lie fallow. But I say, on one condition.'

'Vratch?'

'I think we should try dredge up our Rock Man and restore him as planned. You cannae have a statue to a man for killin the last wolf in Scotland fa didna kill the last wolf in Scotland.'

I studied Vratch's face. Eyes down at her shoes, hands in jeans pockets. A nervous energy like a spring foal about to run for the first time. Twitching.

'Symbols are fine, Vratch. Wolfclaw is a symbol but I don't know if Macqueen killed the last wolf. We can never know that. It's all symbols .'

'It's no *symbols* Ah'm talkin aboot here. Can you spare a Saturday in a fortnight's time? May weekend?'

'OK, aye, sure.'

She looked up. Right through my skull. 'So, see you then.'

Chronicles

The three of us had agreed: go quietly, lie low, lie fallow, stay in touch, change directions. Thus we could agree to Mr Smith's terms. I still had to talk to Ivan and Conger in the next few days. I had told Ivan to relax by taking a few days off. I loaned him my car. Conger was back on his island and I would go out to see him there. I knew our patient had us over a barrel and it was our only way out now. I took heart on one point. CID were deceived by our false Rocky on the hill. We would now have to dredge up the original one in order to insure our deception in case somebody else dredged up the original statue. Its complete restoration could be done at our pace, at our leisure. The weathered replica might fool people for a while – maybe a long time, but it could not last. I'd always thought we had to finish off the Wolfclaw with a final symbolic act and this was the perfect way. Conger would agree. Ivan would be the tricky one. His unyielding loyalty was linked to something deep and enigmatic within him. He would not listen to logic or argument. His family had brought laughter and soul to what had been a grubby pub and were really at home there; because of that I knew Ivan's loyalty to me was unquestioning. He would kill for the happiness of his wife and daughter.

And Vratch? What the hell was she on about? Her idée fixe had become the statue itself. And what was this May Day caper? A picnic, or more? I remembered the hard-set jaw, the determined eyes. It made me nervous.

And I was tired. Twenty years in my old man's country yet I felt outside of everything now. Nor could I ever fully belong to my mother's people. I felt rootless for the first time in my life. I wanted to run away from it all. I remember my mother calling her brother a 'road man'. By this she meant he was a traditionalist, a kind of cultural priest, who encouraged his people to stay on the 'Red Road', the north-south road which he called the real path, the path of life. Any road man should honour his language, customs, people and beliefs by staying on that red road. In contrast, the 'Black Road' was the east-west road which took its traveller far from his true people and culture. The black road had the pitfalls of alcoholism, brutality, compromise, bitterness.

I looked at the comet that night. It was at its brightest, but it was going.

Red Road.

Black Road.

The comet was on its true path. It could travel no other.

But I didn't even know the colour of the road I was on. I didn't even know where the road was. I was lost, with no map.

Chapter twenty-one

I phoned .

'Can I get out to see you tomorrow?'

'Grand. I can fetch you on the shore but I've got some lobster creels to do. Fancy coming along?'

'Great. See you tomorrow morning.'

The day was magic, bright sunshine, blue sky, no breeze. I'd arranged a lift from Killy since Ivan still had my car. The birds were in full throat. The sea was a smooth slate. I could see his small outboard craft coming over from the island.

'Madainn mhath, a bhalaich. De tha' dol?'

'Se la breagha a th' ann.'

'Se gu dearbh.'

'Conger, it's a strange thing thinking in Gaelic. I don't do it easily.'

'Clears the mind, Dan. We'll get your stuff ashore and do some creels.'

It had been three or four years since I'd last been out here. I greeted his folks, both a lot older than I remembered them.

Conger grabbed some sandwiches and a flask.

'Be back in a few hours, folks.'

We got into some oilskins and put the gear in the bow of the aluminium boat – ex-Royal Navy, only reliable in good weather, too light otherwise. Conger fired the outboard and we sped to the leeward side of the island. Conger's buoys lined the island. I straddled a bucket of fresh mackerel and began to slice the fish for creel bait. Conger devised an old partitioned wooden fish box, adding a pile of heavy rubber bands for binding the lobster claws. We went over to the first buoys. Conger cut the engine then pulled the creels. The first creel had two shining lobsters, metallic blue. Conger put the callipers on the lobsters, kept one, the other just measured undersize and he gently dropped it overboard. He banded its claws and put it in the wooden box. I replaced the old bait with a fresh slice of mackerel and began the creel stack. We were soon in a rhythm, lifting the creels, emptying them, re-baiting and stacking. The sea remained smooth. Spring had come to the hills too, and near the shore, we could see the wild primroses. We also heard the first bees of spring buzzing in the yellow whins. Porpoises occasionally broke the surface with lean rainbows. Near the pebble beach, a seal reared up with a small salmon in his mouth. All sealife came up in the creels that day: conger eels, ling, dogfish, haddies, codling, starfish, dog whelks, velvet and green crabs, sea urchins. We caught numerous wrasse with their comical horse teeth. The morning went quickly.

'We'll get these boys into a holding creel then get some lunch.' Conger pointed the boat to the far shore. We sped off to a larger buoy where Conger raised a huge creel and placed our dozen lobsters in it for safe-keeping until further lifting. We then steered for the windward side, sunnier, but the sea slightly rippling. We put in on a shingle beach on a mainland peninsula. We peeled off the oilskins and sat on the warm noonday rocks.

'On a lovely day, Conger, this sea is a great life. With cold beef and mustard pieces and sugared black coffee … life is good, Conger. Cheers, man. The old Wolfclaw seems far away now.'

'What's up then?' asked Conger, aware of the reason for my visit.

'Well, I saw our mysterious injury man in hospital. Recovering. He can't talk but wrote me a note or two.'

Conger was arching a stream of piss into the breeze.

'Symbolic, Dan. Pissing into the wind; pissing into the ocean to make it overflow. So, whose life did we save and was it worth it?'

'Keep pissin into the wind, Conger. We saved the

life of the very same CID man who gave me a verbal thrashing a few weeks ago.'

Conger zipped up. 'How much does he know?'

'I don't know Conger. It's a case of reading between his scribbled lines. He doesn't know the specifics but he has definitely sussed the Wolfclaw. He's clear on Ivan, Vratch and me but doesn't remember anything at all about you and Killy. In fact, he made a few hints about Ivan. In short, he's grateful for his life. He was up there snooping before he fell. He was mostly unconscious but he does remember three clear voices on the hill. It's only a matter of time. Maybe we were just too cocky, too open about the whole thing. He wants us to stop what we're doing and he'll quietly stop his game too. He's not bluffing though. I'm almost afraid to find out how much he really does know.'

'You've told Vratch and Killy?'

'They both agree with me. Make peace with the man, lie fallow, regroup later keep our mouths shut and our options open.'

'And Ivan?'

'I'll see him in a few days. Loaned him my car for a brief holiday.'

'Dan, I'm a fighter. I know what those bastards are like. And like the devil, they have all the best tunes. I think they can only be fought on *their* terms: legal ones. I say give him what he wants in the short term. We still have some options after that. It will get him off our backs and give us a clean slate.'

I felt the beef and mustard on my tongue, coated with the sugared coffee.

'That's exactly how I feel – Rocky Interruptus. I think we all knew this phase would be a short-lived one.'

'Even so, my Glasgow solicitor tells me landholding in the Highlands will never be the same after all these overseas land claims. These are setting a legal precedent, which will alter history in the Highlands. That will outlive us and is entirely legal.'

'You know Conger, that statue. It must have broken up or else sank into a deep pool. We'll never find it but Vratch thinks we should try.'

Conger laughed. 'For Vratch, everything is possible. We should try but we can talk about it later. We've got more creels to do before the wind picks up.'

The sea had begun rippling. Small dark clouds clustered around the hilltops. We had good luck with the creels in the afternoon and added more lobsters to the keeper creel. Conger separated six big haddies. 'Our tea. You're staying the night. I can give you a lift in when I take the lobsters in tomorrow.'

I couldn't argue with that. I hadn't been around a family for many years. In truth, I hadn't eaten a sweet haddie for a long time too.

We each had a hot bath. Conger's old man had filleted the fish and baked them in cream. We ate those with mashed potatoes and later had a dram in front of the fire. Conger's father told me in Gaelic about my own father; their schooldays, their leaving their homeland.

'You dad was a wandering man, a man of the road, even when he was young.' I thought of my mother's phrase: 'road man'. I wondered if my father knew the red road from the black one.

'Your father was always looking west' said Conger's old man. 'Always looking west.'

So, the black road.

I slept on the floor in a sleeping bag, watching the flames lick and die, casting dark shadows over me.

• • • • • • • • • • • • • • • • • •

Next morning, Conger brought me a hot mug of tea and poked the fire into life, throwing a few logs on it. Conger's folks were already at their chores. He was frying up bacon and eggs. Sun streamed in. The door was wide open. Conger did the whole works: tomatoes, mushrooms, toast, coffee.

'We'll be off, Dan, when you're ready but I've got one more thing to show you, in the shed.'

I finished breakfast and went outside. Sunny, still, sea calm. Conger took me to the rear of the house. There was a dry stone building with a corrugated roof.

'This used to be the old wash house.'

It had a small broken window. Light streamed through. Dust danced in the sunbeams. Conger walked to the centre of the room and lifted an old canvas tarpaulin. He lifted it with a great flourish. A sunbeam fell directly on Rocky's head!

Rocky was in two bits. He'd split from the crotch to the oxter on his right side.

Conger chuckled. 'I didn't tell you last night, thinking it would ruin your sleep!'

'Thanks Conger, it would have. How the hell did you retrieve him?'

'Simple. I went at low tide and there he was – pranged on a rock, hooked by each oxter. He was barely visible and wouldn't have been noticed by anyone not looking for him. I wrapped him in a blanket and took him here. He can be stuck together and stuck back up there whenever we feel like it.'

Rocky looked forlorn there, small and dark. Conger covered him again.

'Good night Stony, sweet dreams.'

We climbed into Conger's boat and sped over the sea loch to the holding creel. We lifted it, emptying the lobsters into the fish box, where they breenged harmlessly into one another, their claws secure. Reaching shore, we loaded the box into Conger's pickup and headed for the village.

'Thanks for everything Conger. I needed that sea yesterday. As for Rocky ...'

'Tell Vratch and Killy if you want. How long will the phony statue fool people?'

'I think only the old folk would notice and they rarely get up there except in summer. We'll be OK for a while but a lot depends on how the new stuff weathers.' Conger drove to the pier with his lobsters and I went to Vratch's office. Vratch was on the phone, speaking in Rumanian. She raised an eyebrow as she put down the phone. I whispered.

'Conger rescued Rocky – who is broken but can be healed. He's safe at Conger's.'

Vratch said nothing. She grinned and gave the thumbs up. I phoned Killy from the public phone box. He laughed at the news.

'Our cup of blessings is overflowing,' he said. 'In fact, it is not half-full yet.'

I headed for the hill. Pink and white blossoms, daffodils, crocuses. Hill blazing with yellow gorse. Hills brown with fingers of green, sky pocked with grey-white clouds; sea dimpled. Harbour empty of boats. I was soon at the hilltop. Rocky was convincing. The cement had dried smoothly. The new statue was only a slight shade lighter than the original. Nobody would suspect anything who had no reason to think the original statue was gone. I walked down in late afternoon, feeling more confident and buoyant than I'd been. The visit to Conger's had reminded me what strength there was in the people.

• • • • • • • • • • • • • • • • • •

Chronicles

The broken made whole. Tale of many lives. Lost never found; wounds never healed. Stumbled after, searched for. Broken cleavage of line always there; scars never heal. Physical loss bad enough, what about the soul, volatile and osmotic. Easier to be a stone man, healed by cement or glue; velcro of stone on stone, sand on sand, molecule on molecule. My mother's relatives rarely had all their digits. Fingers and thumbs gone to trap, hook, fire, ice. Hands gone too, and sometimes arms; occupational hazard of hunters, farmers, lumberjacks and sawyers.

A wedge into the log, one blow and the log splits, fibres reaching out from each half.

Killy. Vratch. Ivan. Myself. Striving to bring our halves together. But a soul by definition can not be split. It is immutable, indivisible. Ask Plato. The split is therefore an illusion.

Cree and Gael. Chuvash and Russian. Irish and Gael. Highlander and North Easter. So if that which can't be divided need not be fused, our salvation rests with the stone man, whose restoration is more than putting together just what is already there. When that happens all this seeking stops.

Have you ever held a glass of whisky up to the moon? The moonlight transmutes the amber, giving to the whisky a moon flavour. Try it!

Slainte mhor. Air do shlaint!

Chapter twenty-two

Ivan was back mid-morning, a day earlier than expected. He, Anish and Sura had gone to Aberdeen and returned with a car full of food, clothing and fabric. Ivan gripped me by the left forearm. 'Dan, it is Anish's birthday and we wish you to be our special guest at 7.30 in our flat.'

'You will come, please,' added Sura.

Sura had grown in confidence as her English improved but I realised it was not an easy thing for her to speak to me confidently.

'Of course I will come,' is all I could reply.

'Bring nothing, only yourself,' concluded Ivan.

This made things more difficult because I wanted to persuade Ivan that the Wolfclaw needed to retreat for a time. I also needed to hide our concern for him. Ivan was mercurial but Sura and Anish had settled in well and anything I said to Ivan needed to remain with him for the time being. It would have been better to see Ivan on his own at another time.

I went to the flat about seven. The table was decorated with early garden flowers. The dining room was freshly painted and airy – not at all like the stuffy museum I had remembered. It was a part of the Haddock Arms I rarely went to in the past. The cushions were all in brightly-coloured cases. The two women had on lovely frocks with many brightly-coloured petticoats peeping out. Each had her blonde hair tied back in braids. Ivan was in a long-sleeved peasant blouse. He had on a pair of stunning highly-polished boots. It was such a vibrant and happy family that I felt miserable inside about any involvement Ivan may have had with Wolfclaw and its consequences for him. I was certain he had never told his family about Wolfclaw or its pressures on him. I took a seat at the head of the table. Ivan explained the menu, which he said had been written out on fine paper by Sura. He translated it for me.

Welcome to the Birthday Party of Anish Volkanovna

SOUPS
Borsch (beetroot soup topped with sour cream)
Yublochny (sweet apple soup)
Schi (cabbage soup)
BREAD
Chornya or Belya (black bread or white)
SALAD
Russki Salat (a salad of meat, vegetables and eggs)
MAIN COURSES
Bitochki v smetane (minced veal with sour cream)
Vareschaga (pork and beetroot)
Indeik s vichnovym sousom (turkey plus cherry sauce)
SIDE DISH
Pirozhki (patties made of onion and cabbage)
DESSERT
Kompot (stewed fruit)
Vishniovy (cherries)

The three said a blessing in Chuvashi before the feast. I began with the borsch and black bread. I remember the atmosphere of the meal as much as the food. All eyes smiling at me, numerous toasts, much laughing and singing in Chuvash, Russian and English. Sura brought out a saffron cake and cut a huge slice for me first, then Anish. They sang, then raised vodka in toast. Ivan popped a cassette in the machine and he and Anish waltzed around the room, then Sura signalled me to get up and dance too. Then Ivan did a mad gallop around the room, legs flaying like shuttlecocks while we clapped in time. The floor shook and some of the glasses and bowls rattled on the table. Ivan then stood up and toasted me as the guest of honour:

Here is Dan
Salt to our bread
River to our fish
Earth to our plough
Apple to the bough
We drink to his health
Now.

Anish came back with a bowl of fruit tied in ribbons and kissed me on each cheek. Sura brought in flowers and did the same.

'To Dan, our benefactor.'

Their faces were sparkling and happy. It all hit me in the gut. They were innocents, in a country where darkness and fatalism ruled, qualities we'd always attributed to the Slavic peoples. I also felt I was deceiving them all. I looked at the flickering candles and I thought of cathedrals and refuges, safety and shelter. I had given them that anyway, totally heartsick at Ivan's involvement with Wolfclaw. His loyalty and courage would have been better placed. Then, the mood of the evening changed.

'To Dan, our benefactor,' continued Ivan. 'We asked you here for joy, to thank you. We asked you here for this birthday celebration. You are our friend and protector. You have a soul we understand and you understand our people because your people are the same. But we must also be honest with you. On our trip to the north east, we stopped at a dairy farm to buy cheese. We went on a tour there and asked polite questions of the owners. I told him who I was and introduced him to Anish and Sura. As a young man, the farmer had worked with an overseas agricultural agency and had actually worked in my homeland. We talked and talked about the land there. We stayed for tea. He told me his own stockman is going to branch out with the business so the farmer is looking for another stockman. He would give a house with twenty areas of land. He offered us the house and job: proper jobs with contracts. I told him we could not possibly go as we owe our allegiance to you.'

I looked at their faces, serious now, taut. I read the fierce pride and loyalty there that only I could command, or, release. I knew I had to speak.

'I'm … I'm deeply touched by your own kindness and loyalty. I have always felt that you have given me far more than I have given you …'

Ivan explained some words and phrases that Sura and Anish didn't understand at once.

'You have brought light and laughter to an old pub. You have brought good food and hospitality. The pub is more prosperous than ever, as a result. Look at this room itself – *ochen xorosho-krassivaya* – painted and bright and full of laughter, not cobwebs and depressing shadows. You are people of the land and have brought kindness and decency, appreciated and respected by the whole village. You are New Scots and every nation needs people like you to renew and refresh. No Ivan, you and your family have given so much more than you have taken. It is I who feels the debt.'

I toasted them *Slainte mhor!*

They raised their glasses, faces beaming at my words.

'Now, there is one sadness I haven't spoken of. For many reasons, I no longer wish to work this pub or run it. In fact, I would like to do something else with it. I am young enough to need change in my own life. I will probably sell the pub and leave Macqueensport and it is only your own loyalty which might prevent me from doing this. If you took the jobs in the north east, we would both be free.'

Only briefly, I saw Ivan give me the dark look seen so often in the Wolfclaw, as if to try read my mind, then his face relaxed. He knew it was what I really wanted, not just an excuse to set Ivan free from his obligations to the Haddock Arms.

Then they laughed, blonde pure Chuvashi laughter.

I had made them understand. More food, more drink, more laughter. Ivan and Anish danced, Sura danced with me, pressing close. She had the aroma of fresh fruit: peaches or apples. I could feel the full length of her body – she was almost the same height as me. She kissed me on the lips, laughing more, then kissed me with her tongue and I returned it, also kissing her cheeks and throat. Out of the corner of my eye, I could see Ivan and Anish whirling; they had seen us but both gave the thumbs up. Later, Sura and Anish walked into another room, arm-in-arm. Ivan and I sat facing each other over the table of food and drink, flowers, candles and plates. Ivan poured me a vodka, then poured himself one. He raised it.

'Is this true, Dan, all this about the pub and you going away?'

'I think it is, Ivan.'

'And the Wolfclaw?'

'I've talked … I've talked to the man whose life you saved. He doesn't know much but all the rest of us think we should rest, lie low.'

Ivan hissed. 'Give up?'

'No Ivan. Not stop. Don't forget, you've received letters too.'

'That would never stop me. They could send me back to the Chuvash if they wish. I could survive there now, things have changed.'

Ivan calmed.

'And the job offer in the north east?'

'It is the perfect job for all of us. We love it here but we are land people. Cows. Sheep. Ploughing, growing, harvesting. I would feel more at home but you need us here. We would never consider going there.'

'Does the offer still stand?'

'Yes, for a week but he will not need us at once.'

'Then phone tomorrow, Ivan. You have a future there. By the way, Ivan, our trip up the hill that night was not in vain. Conger has retrieved the statue from the sea and it can be repaired. It is hidden away safely now until we choose to put it back.'

'That makes me feel better, much better. A human life was more than a stone one, but I regretted cutting the statue loose.'

Ivan's face sparkled and he shook my hand furiously.

'I say as a father, too, Dan. Your attentions to Sura would not be discouraged for you are a good and kind man, Dan.'

I blushed. And it was all as simple as that. The Wolfclaw was now unanimous.

Chronicles

I left the room that had once lived and laughed. It was now in the dark, the table mysterious in the moonlight. I was exhausted by my range of emotions: fear, anxiety, concern – for the three people who had pledged their lives to me. It is not easy being a hero. It wrenched my heart to know they would have made the sacrifice of their new life in order to stay loyal to me. I went back to my own room, my mind sizzling. I poured a glass of whisky.

I thought of the aroma of fresh fruit. I remembered dancing with my hands in her hair, running down the curve of her back resting on her buttocks. The soft throbbing of it all, tongues like darting birds. Maybe nothing more, but everything. It was too long since I had felt the mystery of clothing and the softness underneath it.

I propped open my small window, letting in the spring night. A dog barked. I heard the splash of waves on the shore, the occasional hollow knock of a boat or the grinding gears of a fish lorry. The sky was bright, Orion in a new coat. The comet was a milky smudge but further on the horizon. It would soon be lost to vision. A strange delirious living on the earth, so tiny under these stars. The whisky so warming, tingling on the mouth with a sensation, silken, like love.

I slept deeply without dreaming the way daydreamers often do.

Chapter twenty-three

Vratch knocked on the door bright and early on the first of May. She was dressed in jeans and had on a light green blouse. Her black hair was done in ringlets. She had on hiking boots and a huge backpack. 'Got everything we need. Food and drink.'

The sun was blinding, the sea was still, sky a rare perfect blue. We went in Vratch's car, driving about fifteen miles north. We parked in a layby. The loch sparkled, the green-brown hills were bright with broom, loud with bees. Vratch lead the way up the burn. We walked for ten minutes or so, not speaking. The ground underfoot was rough peat hag, squelching as we walked.

'A rest here?' Vratch tossed me a tangerine, taking one for herself. We sat on a warm boulder. 'So, Vratch, you know where we're going and why?'

'I ken an aa. Ever been up here before?'

'Many years ago I walked up the burn to a pool where the burn widened. I caught a huge pike there. I threw a spinner into the pool and the pike hit. He leapt trying to shake the spinner free but I finally got him up on the bracken. He looked like a tiger with jade and black stripes. I let him go. I remember wondering how far up the burn went, and remember seeing some old shielings further up. I could see smaller lochans as well.'

Vratch put the peels into her pack, taking mine too. She wiped the juice from her mouth with the back of her hand.

'Did you talk to our hospital patient?'

'I did, before he was discharged last week. He was a lot better and could speak properly. We shook hands on our original bargain. We stop, he stops, all is forgotten, wiped from the record. He was thinking adieu, I was thinking au revoir. Fallow, but not forever fallow.'

'And Ivan?'

'Ivan has been offered a good stockman's job in the north east. I encouraged him to go because I might be selling off the Haddock Arms in the future.'

Vratch looked sidelong at me. 'Is that true, Dan?'

'It could be Vratch, it could be. I've been restless lately but that's because Wolfclaw has dominated all my thoughts so far.'

'Ah ken, ah ken.'

'I can see for you, Vratch, being here is being home after being so long in the north east. For me, I'm not sure. The whole Wolfclaw business has taken me down some different mental roads. Memories of my mother and her people. I'm less sure about some things.'

'Such as?'

'Look around us. Lochs, hills, birds, fish. Freedom is *here*. What was the Wolfclaw fuss about? It almost got a man killed.'

'Aye, but we could be kicked off this land at a rich man's whim because of deer, fish, grouse. Someone may be spying on us right now through the telescope of a deer rifle.'

'But politics and nationality are only a part of life, not all of it. We were put here to enjoy life too.'

Vratch got up, dusting off her jeans. She stretched like a big cat. Her blouse hitched up, showing a tanned flat stomach. We were walking on perfectly rounded stones all of the same size. The bracken smelled like sweet hay. The water was the colour of churning milk from the snowmelt higher up the valley. The burn hissed as it rushed through the hard green reeds. Vratch pointed to the left where two huge adders sunned themselves on a flat stone. I remembered these places on the way to the Pike Pool. The Green-Grey Loch, Rough Burn, Rough Loch, Loch of the Ribbon Spout, Loch of the Big Trout, The Valley of the Broken Moor. Primroses covered the cliff on the opposite side of the burn. Our vista narrowed as we went further up the glacial valley. The pools were sheltered and still. Trout came up for larvae and flies on the surface. Tadpoles wriggled from spawn in some of the rock pools. At the end of the loch were two crumbling shielings in a meadow of pink and purple purslane. The sunlight turned all the still waters into prisms. The meadow disappeared into the rocky foothills leading to the next staircase loch. We could see for miles in the direction we'd already come but our vista ahead was narrowed by the deep gorge. The hill was covered in small rivulets and waterfalls. We had just left the Glen of the Broken Moor, entering the Glen of the Hunter. The ruined shielings were at the end of a small loch in a meadow; the grass was dry and spongy from the heat and sun. We'd walked for three hours already.

'Fancy some lunch?' said Vratch, motioning to the shieling. The ground there was soft, the grass ankle deep and dry. Vratch put her backpack down and took out a blanket, spreading it on the grass floor of the shieling. We spread out the food and drink. Red wine, corkscrew, sandwiches, fruit, juice, nuts, a flask of coffee. We drank the wine from the Thermos cups and ate some of the sandwiches. The sky over the ruin was bright blue and cloudless. We cleared the picnic things and lay side-by-side on our backs. Wine, heat, bees buzzing. We were both tired and dozed off.

• • • • • • • • • • • • • • • • • •

I awoke to Vratch's curls hanging down like a dark waterfall. She had rolled over above me and begun kissing my face. I returned the kisses, feeling her stretch herself the length of my body. Vratch sat up, her knees between my legs. She unbuttoned her green blouse and unhooked her bra, quickly throwing them in the grass. She leaned forward again, putting her left breast to my mouth. I felt the nipple stiffen, and kissed and licked each one. Vratch helped me peel my shirt off and unbuckle my belt. Vratch then stood up and unbuckled her own jeans. She let her knickers fall down and stripped off her socks. Both naked, we rolled gently on the warm blanket and Vratch guided me into her slowly. I remember the blue sky and her dark hair under the heat of birdsong. Drowsy bees buzzed in the meadow. We melted together and fell asleep.

• • • • • • • • • • • • • • • • • •

We woke up an hour or so later. It was early afternoon. Vratch's head was against my chest. She was grinning. 'We both needed *that.*' Her fingers traced my mouth. She kissed me again and sat up.

'That's one of my reasons for bringing you here. Now I'll show you the other reason.'

Vratch put on her socks, knickers, jeans and blouse. She brought my clothes over to me. I dressed slowly, wondering what encore could possibly follow. We walked hand in hand for a distance, letting go when the glen narrowed, and the rocky path became steeper. For over an hour, we climbed around deep pools and waterfalls. It was magic, truly a lost corrie not visible from any direction but the air. It was colder here, sheltered from the sun. Vratch lead the way. I was hypnotised by her movements. Less than an hour ago, I had entered that body, filled it, felt the curve and warmth of it beneath me. That strange, strange creature was now balancing on cold rock, climbing into a glacial scar. We stopped to put jumpers on. Vratch pulled me over and ran her lips over my face. I felt an erection like a standing stone. She squeezed it, laughing.

'Alpha male, meet alpha female.'

'Are we coming to an encore?'

'Ken, one better than sex and we're almost there.'

Vratch produced a compass.

'Ah ken fine but ah want tae mak siccar. There are several corries to the left but they all look the same. We have to get the right one.'

We walked on the wet stone to the left of the snowmelt burn, which foamed into small pools and waterfalls. The sky was not clearly visible above the sheer sandstone cliffs, dotted with spindly birches and rowans. Vratch put her fingers to her lips and began crouching forward, signalling me to do the same. We both slipped, cracking our knees on the wet rock. Our jeans were soaking from walking through deeper pools. We walked upstream, the water almost knee-deep in places, Vratch and I being the same height. Out of the sun, it was freezing. We continued this way for fifteen minutes. Vratch motioned me down again. 'Time for the encore' she whispered, grinning. Vratch pointed to the far ledge and caught my eye to make sure I was seeing what she was pointing at. She was right. What I saw was better than sex – even sex with the pointer herself!

• • • • • • • • • • • • • • • • • •

The bright sun forced my eyes to adjust to the dark cliffs. I saw a grey ghost, just a faded outline against the cold rock. A large wolf stood on the ledge which formed the front rim of a small cave. Vratch quietly handed me a pair of binoculars and I could make out some small wolf cubs in the cave. Vratch and I did not speak but watched the she-wolf pacing, sniffing the air. We were downwind and well camouflaged. I think she knew we were there but were not a threat to her den. The wolf was nervous, twitching. We could not go any closer. We could hear our hearts pounding, even above the sound of the rushing burn. We watched for a long time, until the cubs came further out and we could clearly count four of them. The she-wolf, her eyes bright yellow against the grey rock, lowered her head and while the cubs bounded into the cave. Vratch motioned me to retreat and we didn't speak until we were well down the burn. A few hours brought us back to the shieling meadow, still warm in a sinking sun, a world far away away from the one we had just seen. We went back to the shieling. Vratch unloaded her backpack, while I emptied my smaller rucksack. Vratch got a fire going from dry wood and heather stems. I boiled up a pot of tea on my small gas stove. Vratch had spread a tent out on the grass.

'So Dan, better than sex, eh?'

'As good as, as good as ... ' We laughed.

'Vratch, how long did you know wolves were here?'

'Three years ago, when I came back from the north east. I used to hike here a lot but one day I took a wrong turn. I had my compass so could pinpoint exactly where it was later. I saw both the male and female on the ledge above me and I later heard them howling. The male was much bigger and darker. I've heard there are usually three or four cubs born in April or May so that was a normal group we saw back there. Packs average five to fifteen, so there are probably more wolves than we've seen.'

'Do you think they have always been there, Vratch?'

'I think so, unless this is a secret wildlife experiment. But those wolves looked canny and wild.'

'And if here, why not the Cairngorms, the Trossachs, the Nevis Range and so on?'

'Now you understand the looks I was giving you at the Wolfclaw meetings every time Macqueen's name came up. This whole town was founded on a lie – the way we lie about alcoholism, agoraphobia, wife-battering, child-beating – all under the shadow of a man who is remembered for a bad deed, moreover, one he didn't even do. Lies. Lies.'

'We can't tell anyone.'

'No. Crofters, gamekeepers and the tourist boards would go mental. Those wolves have only survived because of their isolation. This strath is too rough for stalking. Deer herds couldn't find food up there. There are no grouse or salmon. The big pike have kept trout numbers down and much of the water is too rough for angling anyway. There are so many good hills up the main strath that hikers and climbers never go up the side cuts. The path is slippery and dangerous and you saw how cold it gets back there, even on a warm day. Anybody stumbling up there would make so much noise on the way the wolves would take cover. The pack can feed. Rabbits, hares, ptarmigan, wildfowl, voles, rats, the odd deer. I think they have survived forever up there.'

'Who else might know?'

'Only the two of us.'

'Vratch, will we tell the rest of the Wolfclaw?'

'Ken, I think we can now.'

'Then why *me* Vratch? Why did you tell me?'

'Trust. Maybe I thought you'd earned this more, would understand it best. Anyway, two seductions for the price of one. I'm no good at indirect approaches. It's cool the nicht.'

We snuggled into one sleeping bag in the tent. We left the fire burning. Vratch's hair smelled of heather smoke.

• • • • • • • • • • • • • • • • • •

Canis lupus. Order, Carnivora. Family, Canidae. Largest member of the Canidae family. White, black, tan, grey and all shades and combinations. Residual populations in Nearctic and Palaearctic regions, mistakenly thought extinct in some of those regions. Many subspecies. Brains one third bigger than an intelligent dog's. Can be taught to undo locks and manage gate bolts. We told the rest of the Wolfclaw and the reaction was the same: disbelief, belief, laughter, then pure joy. All of us felt freed, vindicated, nothing else mattered. This was not symbolic, nor was it illegal. The statue could wait until the new millennium. Ivan, Anish and Sura left yesterday for their new life in the north east. Their flat is clean but lifeless now. The day they left, Sura and Anish kissed me, Sura lingering a bit longer. Ivan lifted me in a huge bear hug, lifting me off my feet. Then he pushed me at arms length. He presented me with his mackerel knife and his tobacco pouch made of mammoth fur. I know that meant more to him than anything. They walked out on a warm summer's day. I promised to visit those New Scots who would give so much to this land. Whenever I smell apples or peaches, I will think of tall blonde Sura dancing under the comets.

Later, Vratch needed a place so I promised the flat to her.

They were like ghosts those wolves, ghosts but always there, destroying our shabby lies and assumptions.

Love. Lips, cheeks, thighs, bellies, legs, eyes. I'd forgotten what living was like.

i.
We are not ghosts
or shadows on cold rock,
but denim on denim,
tongue on skin,
skin on cotton.
Hearts of bleeding tides,
ebbing, surging,
in creeks of mystery.
Utopia under a dying sun,
frothing snowmelt,
Winter's cold milk,
adders swelling with spring,
bees suck warm forbidden places.

ii.
The wolf was pale ice, frozen
smoke. Wolf cub eyes are blue,
turn yellow with age.
Feet padded like a child's
outlandish slippers.
Moving water protects
against ghosts.
Our hearts howl silence,
our human pack begs an answer.
Even comets look like wolf claws.

iii.
Melting moon,
when your drips cool,
they harden into primroses.

(Why do you weep Dan, it will not change anything.
Ghost, that is exactly why I weep.)

Chapter twenty-four

We called it 'fallow', rest and recuperation, healing, staring into the black hole of the millennium.

> Killy: Strange days, Wolfclaw. What did we really do? Cling to a faith, the old faith. Faith is always loyalty to the Unseen: the Sweet County Mayo or the rock where I now stand. I belong to the oldest faith on earth: the faith of planters, sowers, gardeners, seed droppers, nurturers. The oak trees I now plant I will never live to see in their full glory. They will be ripped by rabbits, sheep, deer and salt-wind. The wind will tease them, let them grow firm enough only to snap them like dry bones. I remember telling my children my dream, my vision of the oak planter, a version of the Johnny Appleseed story, but instead, planting acorns from Ardnamurchan to John O'Groats. My brother-in-law took a job as a consultant in Edinburgh so Rowena and I bought out his business and premises and it's going well. Good work for a family and a good living for one man. On weekends we load up the van with fishing rods and picnics and we go plant oak trees, protecting and fencing them. The girls have named each site and they keep careful records of its growth and progress. So far our groves are: Elva, Lugh, Neesha, Uisnach, Ardan, Roughred, Concobar, Deirdre, Derdriu (the Oak Prophet), Ainlle, Cormac and Dubthach. We laugh about what will come. Maybe in a colder, drier time, maybe in a warmer, wetter one oak groves all over the Highlands will shelter wild boars again to root and seed the ground. Better, will lovelorn poets, harpers and lovedaft youths seek shelter from wind and rain in a kind green human place after so much desolation? Bringing green back to grey, green the living colour, spring again. A ghradh, there is plenty room for music and laughter here; much much more than now. Have you ever held an acorn in your hand? Crushed one, eaten it? A whole universe in a seed. Wolves will howl under those

trees one day. I will paraphrase Sir Boyle Roche again:

'My cup of joy is overflowing, in fact, it is not half full yet.'

Tri aois firein, aois craoibh dharaich.

Thrice the eagle's age, the age of the oak tree.

And the deer was thought to live thrice a man's life and the eagle, thrice a deer's.

But if we live well, we live long enough.

Dia's Mhuire dhuit agus Padraig!

Conger: I could only laugh and dribble like a mad man when I heard Vratch and Dan tell me about the wolves. I am Highland, a Gael. I don't believe in the 'last' of anything. Last Wolf, Last Gaelic Speaker, Last Survivor. Last to be born on the island, last to leave the island, last inhabited island. Dan understands, and Vratch. Ivan because he lost his homeland, Killy, because he left it. Man, surely us believing in the last wolf helped keep it alive and then who would have found it? Alexander Carmichael, the folklorist once met an old man in Sutherland in the nineteenth century who claimed to have seen bears alive in Sutherland in his own lifetime. It is impossible, therefore I believe.

Aithnicher an leomhann air sgriob de ionga. The lion is known by a scratch of his claw; so is the wolf.

The Wolfclaw was never a diversion for me. It was *serious play*. The battle on this island is twofold: against wind, rain, rats. Against: rules, bureaucrats, quangos, landlords. *Human rats*. These are trying to turn us against each other (only three people on so much land, and two of those old people) and against the birds and trees which we have nurtured and maintained in the teeth of winds (and rats); there is as much harmony on this island as anywhere in the Highlands where all life is a threatened species. The larks of my youth are gone, so are the sea trout. Wolfclaw let me have some pride, let me get some of my own back. It made some squirm the way I have squirmed. It built my confidence and 'tactical' awareness. No real harm could come to me; a few days in jail, a fine or two. The great legacy of the Wolfclaw is the legal one against eviction and past Clearances. The is no statute of limitation against cruelty and we are proving it in the courts. The case is snowballing, claims arc coming in from thousands all over the world.

Restoration? I restored my pride: in my own people and those like Killy and Ivan who would help us. I made four good friends for life who shared a dream with me for a brief time. Vratch? Vratch is with Dan now, a good choice for her. My nightly dreams of my Wolfclaw sister were not brotherly dreams I'm afraid. They were the dreams of a rake, a tomcat, but at least they were never nightmares. Sometimes I thought of Wolfclaw retreating to this island. Ivan and his family as well. In early Christian times, this island supported two hundred people. Killy could come too, covering the island in oak trees again. The early Irish monks arrived here in boats of oak which they then took apart to make chapels with. We would have our own village hall, school and graveyard. Our own songs and poems; we could grow apples and crops, raise fruit. Keep cattle. That probably could not happen; passions and obsessions would be magnified. We would lose our friendship.

I haven't forgotten the man in the old washing shed either. He'll be wrapped up and taken to the mainland, down to our mysterious surgeon-sculptor. Old Macqueen will carry his wolf or two when the time is right. The millennium is coming to remind us that the world is not coming to an end; it is coming to a beginning.

• • • • • • • • • • • • • • • • • • •

Ivan: How different is this land and people. The north east. So unlike the west, but so like my native land. The soil is like thick pudding, feeding wheat, barley, oats and potatoes – all old friends of mine. The rivers are teeming with fish. There are trees and forests. The oak is my father, the birch my mother, so we sang, so we sing. I watch these lapwings, these crazy crippled birds fly like leaves in an angry wind. Anish and Sura are very happy here, back on the land. They have here as much of the Chuvash as they will ever have in another country. Cows. I was born with them. They have souls. Milk turned into butter and cheese is as magic as turning coal into diamonds, granite into gold. The trees top the hills like rooster combs, snipped by the wind. Sura says the trees are hedgehogs. I am paid well, treated like a man. I have my own house and land. Sura has already 'i spik o i laan, ken?' Oaks, birches, rowans, elms, walnuts. Wolves should be here, feeding on rabbits and pheasants. Moon. Trees. Fields. Wolf under the moon, shadow on the hill. I am a free man because I am on the land; a mackerel cutter on the land. The Wolfclaw saved me and I was fated to save the life of a man on the hill, who would have not been there but for the Wolfclaw. All things in their time. Those good people saved me because they took me in. They gave me hope. And Cree Dan who does not know the strength of his own soul, cloven in two. When he merges those half-souls together, he will be powerful beyond his dreams. His kindness will never be forgotten. Even my daughter may have been his if he had wished. She is young but knows her own heart. 'Papa, he was not ready. I will not blame him for this. He is twice my age but is not yet half of what I know. He is off on a road, like one of those bearded Russian holy men who used to beg grain from us. I know all this from a kiss – or two.'

He must learn more of his mother's people. She lived, like us, on the cold belt of the northern world. Our animals and trees are the same. Our Shamen are the same. If Dan is with Vratch, his soul will be healed with fire, the way fine horse shoes are. She was the bravest of us, had the movement, sight and sense of a wolf. So unlike my own people, though. Could she read minds through her dark curls, those nights at the Haddock Arms in that room of stuffed animals? Vratch, that nervous grin.

And the wolves: Who else but her could ever have found them? Who else? The wolves in my homeland are not dead yet but they are hunted. For all of us it was like finding a god or a unicorn, a griffin or a centaur. The Scots. They are like the good wolf. They are a pack, a tribe, they are so canny, so intelligent. They have a gentle wildness they are ashamed of. They don't even see it within themselves. I must have seemed a giant ignorant man, a peasant, nodding and laughing at all the wrong times. They did not know how much I struggled to find the right words for my thoughts. How many words does a man need? Chuvash, Russian, English, Scots. I learned a word: 'inarticulate'. We were really all the same though, looking for a surface to cover the depths, looking for a name for a feeling.

Cree Dan understood my feelings more than the others. That's why I gave him my mackerel knife, a symbol of my loyalty to the clan. I also gave him the pouch made of mammoth fur. It was the most valuable thing I owned. They think I was joking that night in the Haddock Arms but I was deathly serious. I would have cut my whole manhood off, then slit my throat in the same knife motion. We Chuvash people survived for a millennium by sometimes turning our ploughshares into daggers.

• • • • • • • • • • • • • • • • • •

Vratch: A 'comely lass' they called me. The rewards for being comely are sometimes not comely. Men brush up against me, grope me, run their hands up my skirt and undress me with their eyes, even in the village where I was born. Creepy, flatulent men, commercial men, cold and blubbery like the haddies and coddies I work with every day. Fish? Ah'll hae nae mair o fish. Ahm fished oot. My old man is a Gael, sometime church elder, and still beats my mother. I told him: 'One more time and I'll have the police in.' He called me an Aiberdeen slut and said that I should know all about the police after my filthy public demonstration which disgraced the family.

'And you sleeping with that bartender, too.' My mother was scurrying around with her apron on, up to elbows in flour, rolling out dough for HIS tea, at 11am!

'Ma, use that rollin pin on his heid. Et couldnae dae ony hairm.'

Wolfclaw, brilliant. I knew about the wolves before then, became obsessed with them. I drew power from them like one of those 'comely' Victorian spinsters who invested their sexual urges in secret gardens, playmates, magical cupboards, horses. Please no psychology: alpha male and alpha female. My own hierarchy at home, crouching before the claw and fang: absolute power. So when the Wolfclaw was born, I knew something beyond me was in motion, maybe the planets, the third millennium, fa kens? I needed different friends too, Ah kent all the lassies here, an aa kent me. I needed men who would leave me alone. I knew *the look*, not from Killy, maybe from Conger and Cree Dan, though they tried to conceal it. And I was not entirely right in my head at the time. Fish. Dead. Cold. Eyes glossed over, blood, guts. Selling death daily in five languages. I was tired.

That day on the river bank I was frightened to death. I was shaking inside. I stood my ground to the big men. At that moment I thought I was arresting that Fist everywhere; that black eye, split lip, cauliflower ear.

She is dark but she is comely. No buts.

And Dan, he knows what it means to be and not to be, in a homeland between language and culture. He is a gentle and good man, yet a boy, alas a brother (and sometimes *all* I wanted was something hard and filling inside me). Trouble was, he would have never made any move at all. Seduction right down to the sandwiches, coffee and blanket. Ah needed that, sisters, ken?

Restoration? We will all get back our limbs and souls. Macqueen was a sorry little prick, hangman on the hills. Pointer tae whit? The last wolf, my marble-hued arse! I thought once we should have blown him to bits, put an end to a sorry little lie and all the lies that stink up this place: alcoholism, violence, low-flying, sabbatarianism. It all fuckin stinks, like rotten mackerel. Lies. Lies. Lies. For me, the last act is when that stone man cradles a wolf cub in his arms, then we can truly begin to get away from that lie, that vicious cycle. We cleared the wolf, then were cleared ourselves. We hunted, then were hunted. They broke up our tribe, our pack and we turned to snarling loners and suspicious vagrants on our own land.

The Haddock Arms:

Sawdust and burnished Canadian pitch pine brought back from Newfoundland as ballast, salt-soaked, sealed with seasickness and homesickness, and shellacked with sweat and blood. This hotel an archaeologist's dustbin, each fixture; brass, formica, plastic, bakelite. From a crusty whoreson of a whaler, a harpoonist's den to a suburban plastic chintz. Woodworm gone for chintz. Twee candles in netted candle holders. Frozen scampi, frozen chips, frozen peas. TV in the corner. Stuffed salmon, fat ferox, peacock feathers, stuffed wildcats and pine martens pushed to frontiers, into cupboards and storerooms and cubby holes. So a century and a half from fifty pound silver salmon to formica and all visitors and locals caught in a timewarp. Sweating on upholstery saturated with memories, perfume, cheap deodorant, wafted over with the smell of farts, spilled drink, piss and puke, slopped with every off-key ballad and country western song, twanged in Scots, American and Gaelic. An unwritten history of erections, twitches, pulsations, hands held, thighs groped, zippers unzipped, silk and cotton and: windows broken, jaws cracked, eyes blackened, thumbs unsocketed and swearing and damning to hell in a dozen languages.

Then paint, polish, wax, stain and varnish. Wood exposed, stripped, glistening. Gone the plastic and formica, gone the TV and jukebox. Enter fresh haddock, crab and lobster, venison, rabbit, birch wine, rowan jelly, trout, salmon, charr and pike and everything grown in back gardens of rich soil brought back for centuries also as ballast (from Ireland). And one man with two souls and a woman with many more souls than that now living in the place, lighting fine cracking fires.

Cree Dan: on the millennium: Some would like a tearing of the earth, floods, volcanoes, earthquakes. But that is happening already, has always been happening, this rending of the earth. A real millennium would be to *stop* rending and tearing the earth. There are many here who come at exactly the same time every night: a few half-pints, leave exactly at the same time to go home to a fixed tea, like a menu, on every night of the week. These would still queue up on Apocalypse Eve and go home for their tea: meat and two vegetables.

1000AD. The Maya and Central American civilisations had universities, computers, schools of philosophy and astrophysics while the peasants of Europe panicked, purged themselves with flagellation and orgies or hunted down the Jews in their midst. Nobody can yet reckon how many Jews died in 1000AD. People fled to caves, followed skeletal lunatics to deserts. Then the next day came, they dusted themselves and got ready for the next thousand years.

A Messiah? Where would a Messiah even begin? White horse, pale horse, black horse, red horse. Mountains and straths moved, islands drowned, portents of locusts, falling stars, smoke, theft, fornication, murder. Read the news. Every day is the Last Day.

I agree and repent. *Oh, I repent.* But what will we do? We are lying in wait, like the poor stone man in Conger's island shed.

Me:
Foetus, baby, boy, man, skeleton.

Chapter twenty-four

Tree: I would be an oak.
Fish: I would be a salmon.
Animal: I would be a wolf.
Bird: I would be an eagle.
Colour: I would be green.
Stone: Red sandstone.
Wind: North, winter.
Earth: Prairie dust.
Fire: Lightning.
Star: Pole star.
Song: Coyote, on red dust.
Love: I have that now, dark and comely.

The Haddock Arms, dispensing poison and happiness in the same measure.

Delicate scale, men walk in but crawl out like bairns. How about a museum to the history of lies, of things we believe in or don't believe in? Or, The Museum of the Last of Anything. Unicorns, Loch monsters, big cats, sea serpents? Vratch has a better idea. A hostel for the walking wounded of the Highlands: unpublished novelists and dysfunctional poets.

Cree Dan: *Sorry Vratch, the Haddock Arms is no big enough. We'd have to rent Hampden.*

Chapter twenty-five

Two days before millennium eve Vratch and I saddled up two horses and rode to the ruined shielings in the Wolf Strath. My horse was red, Vratch's horse was white. I could have borrowed two more horses, one for Killy and Conger. Those two riders would not leave their families on Hogmanay, to say nothing of the end of the world. So Vratch and I became the Two Horseriders of the Apocalypse. Vratch and I knew horses well enough. We left at dawn, when mist rose from the loch. Everywhere was silent except for the steady squelch of the horses' hooves. We had packed everything we needed and were able to pack extra gear on the horses. We covered the distance easily and quickly. The horses had been used for stag culling and were steady walkers, strong and controlled. We arrived at the shielings at noon, unloaded and pitched our tent, built a ring of stones for our fire and unloaded all our food and drink into the smaller tent. One day before the end of the world we screwed each other silly all day (with rest and drink in between) on the assumption that the rending of heaven and earth would be the grandest *coitus interruptus* ever. In the beating of hearts and the warm coming together, the tingling of life from toenail to the grey sheaths of the brain, the eternal moment, destroying universes and dying many times.

'So Vratch, the last day of 1999 and the end of our cruel time and with it, the Second Coming. If a man or woman have one day to live, how live it?'

'You've answered your own question, loverboy. A poem, a song, the making of children.'

'The end of the world is also supposed to be a restoration of it.'

We sat in the shieling on that sunny December day. A fire blazed in the centre of the ruin. Our tent was pitched in the corner, the walls of the building shielding us from the prevailing winds – calm at the moment. We boiled our tea in my small gas stove. Vratch was frying up some bacon and eggs. The skies were riddled blue and white. I thought of the dark brown trout ascending the burn into quieter pools to drop their eggs and milt. Not hungry, not diverted from this life-dance on the last day of the earth; dark instinct, the power of life. I could not tell Vratch how I would weep to think of these hills no more, these burns and lochs, these leaping muscular fish that had survived here since the last Ice Age, when this land was gouged and clawed along its spine; that the overhead eagles and buzzards would no more swoop for rabbits and hares, that the wolves up the hidden strath would no longer howl.

We ate quickly, the bacon salty on the tongue, the coffee erasing the salt. Our horses grazed quietly on the sweet grass of the other shieling, red horse and pale horse. The afternoon slid quickly into dark. Vratch had a great pot of venison stew going: carrots, spuds, onions, sweet suet dumplings. We had a few bottles of whisky stored, a bottle of local malt lay on the grass, catching the firelight. The sky was clear and bright, Orion studded and proud. We had no idea of the time. The fire sparked and spat, flames casting shadows even further.

'So Vratch, how will it all end? What does your intuition tell you?'

'We need seven angels breaking seven seals. We need four horsemen and we've only got one. I'm a horsewoman. We also need some prophecies, ken?'

Ken.

The night wore on. We jumped when we first heard the mournful, low, repeating howl. The wolves began to howl, solitary, then one to another, muted by the rock and water and by a rising wind. We shivered and held hands. Vratch started a low growl too, her face creased in joy and fun and then she howled and I picked it up. We heard the wolves pause, for a long time or only seconds, as if to register our timbre and pitch, register our pack, then they returned the howl, softly and less sure, howling in a New Age. Our horses stamped and twitched from a vestigial fear of something deep within them, something they had never heard but remembered. They soon relaxed. Vratch and I could hear them munching and whinnying. We saw their breath on the cold air.

• • • • • • • • • • • • • • • • • •

On the last night of the earth, we heard great fish splashing in the loch. We saw our human breath under Orion, under a million dying stars and journeying comets. And the prophets came, as we knew they would, to hunker down for whisky and stew and the good crack. They came from the night and disappeared back into the night. Bakunin strong and dark, Michael Davitt – I mind Vratch holding out her left hand to shake his left hand – she'd remembered Davitt had lost his right arm at the age of eleven in a Lancashire cotton mill. He looked tired, haggard under his thinning black hair and short beard. Isabella Gunn helped herself to bread and stew, cocked her head wildly at the wolf howling. Donnchaidh Ban and McCodrum, some of the great Land Leaguers and Fenians; all sat at our fire. Vratch and I had time too. We both agreed the Stone Man could wait; our own fallow time could take us to Cree Country, Lapland, Siberia, Greenland, where I could know more about half of my soul. The Haddock Arms needed restored too, not physically. I told Vratch about the Shaking Tent, the arctic ritual where a person confronts his soul in a tent but exits an altered person; this confrontation is not done for personal reasons but for the welfare of the tribe.

Vratch said we had already been in the shaking tent and that things would not be the same after that great shaking!

'There are many kinds of out-of-body experiences, let's go have one.'

We smoored the fire.

• • • • • • • • • • • • • • • • • •

The Night of the Prophets

Bakunin:

The poetry, music and art of the millennium will be rooted in the passion of destruction. Men, women and children of the world will no longer accept hunger and disease; poetry and music of mere observation will be a luxury. There will be black poets, red poets and yellow musicians who will tap the depths of destruction. Poetry will then be a phoenix; the greatest of these poets, painters and musicians will come from war-torn countries girt by mountains and sea.

Michael Davitt:

An heir of mine, also a one-armed man, will point the way and one arm will be enough. People all over the world will claim back their land. It will be the people's land and the great landthieves will melt away. Spies and bailiffs will seek other work. This great one-armed man will have forebears from County Mayo. His forebears crossed oceans and jungles to the southern hemisphere. After unsettled times, every man will have land and the means to it. Before that will be a drought and the wind will be sour with rich top soil, blown to the corners of the earth, just like my people. Ireland will be healed, its wounds will be salved.

Isabella Gunn:

Buckskin will be the fashion of the rich. Women will shoot, men will iron. When seven women rule seven great nations, peace and comfort will come. Women will feed and clothe the world, men will learn to nurse and heal. Lone mothers will no longer be ridiculed and persecuted as I was; no longer treated as madwomen to be buried in paupers' graves. Orkney will become the centre of the universe and will give birth to ten thousand musicians.

John Murdoch:
It will be Sutherland or Ross-shire, or the great rough Bounds of Argyll. It will begin with one song. This song will sweep all before it; it will unite the people. Uniting them to say no. The politicians will have no choice but to solve the land issue once and for all. There will be no bloodshed. It will be a song. 'Just' a song.

Murdoch was impressive at the fire, his great beard casting long shadows and his eyes catching the glint of the firelight.

Donald MacLeod:
These ruins bring back powerful memories. As a stonemason, I put my faith in stone. No more roofs will come down now, and many roofs will go back up. Men, women and children driven from rocky lands to lands of clay, wood and sand will return through their descendants. The diaspora will cease and reverse, like a river halting its flow and flowing against its own current until its very course is altered. Many rivers in Scotland will reverse their flow when this time comes. Too late for many whose bitterness is harder than granite. And stone? The statues will come down and only a few will go back up. Cattle will return and people will return to shielings. Everything will be restored. Gaelic will be spoken by the people again and the auld religion will gain ground. The salmon will be the people's fish once more.

MacLeod waved and seemed to fade into the stone of the shieling.

Then, the dawn came. Vratch and I watched the salmon-pink clouds slip in as the cold mist rose from the still loch. The horses snorted, stretching as they grazed, their breath clouding above the frozen earth. We cleared the old ash from the fire, then blew the living embers into flame. We ate breakfast, dusted off, and in the first morning after the long night, we began to walk up the dark strath.

 Publishing October 2000

The Wolfclaw Chronicles
Tom Bryan
A powerful debut novel bridging the cultures of Ireland, Russia, Canada, Scotland and England.
ISBN 1-903238-10-2
Price £9.99

Rousseau Moon
David Cameron
Lyrical, intense, sensitive, foreboding – a remarkable first collection.
ISBN 1-903238-15-3
Price £9.99

Life Drawing
Linda Cracknell
The eagerly awaited first collection from an award-winning writer.
ISBN 1-903238-13-7
Price £9.99

Hi Bonnybrig & Other Greetings
Shug Hanlan
Strikingly original short stories and a very funny novella.
ISBN 1-903238-16-1
Price £9.99

The Tin Man
Martin Shannon
A debut novel from a new and exciting young writer.
ISBN 1-903238-11-0
Price £9.99

Occasional Demons
Raymond Soltysek
A dark, menacing and quite dazzling collection from one of Scotland's most talented new writers.
ISBN 1-903238-12-9
Price £9.99

About 11:9

Who makes the decisions?

11:9 titles are selected by an editorial board of six people: Douglas Gifford, Professor and Head of Department of Scottish Literature, University of Glasgow; Donny O'Rourke, poet, lecturer and journalist; Paul Pender, screenwriter and independent film producer; Jan Rutherford, specialist in book marketing and promotion; Marion Sinclair, former editorial director of Polygon and lecturer in publishing and Neil Wilson, managing director of 11:9.

Our aims

Supported by the Scottish Arts Council National Lottery Fund and partnership funding, 11:9 publish the work of writers both unknown and established, living and working in Scotland or from a Scottish background.

11:9's brief is to publish contemporary literary novels, and is actively searching for new talent. If you wish to submit work send an introductory letter, a brief synopsis of your novel, a biographical note about yourself and two typed sample chapters to: Editorial Administrator, 11:9, Neil Wilson Publishing Ltd, Suite 303a, The Pentagon Centre, 36 Washington Street, Glasgow, G3 8AZ. Details are also available from our website at **www.11-9.co.uk.**

If you would like to be added to a mailing list about future publications, either register on our website or send your name and address to 11:9, Neil Wilson Publishing Ltd, Suite 303a, The Pentagon Centre, 36 Washington Street, Glasgow, G3 8AZ.

11:9 refers to 11 September 1997 when the Scottish people voted to re-establish their parliament in Edinburgh